Now a...
**Har...**
ro...
by An...
con...
on the movie scre...

starring
# KEIR DULLEA · SUSAN PENHALIGON

*Leopard*
*in the*
*Snow*

Guest Stars
# KENNETH MORE · BILLIE WHITELAW

featuring GORDON THOMSON as MICHAEL
and JEREMY KEMP as BOLT

Produced by JOHN QUESTED and CHRIS HARROP
Screenplay by ANNE MATHER and JILL HYEM
Directed by GERRY O'HARA
An Anglo-Canadian Co-Production

OTHER

by JANE DONNELLY

Many of these titles are available at your local bookseller,
or through the Harlequin Reader Service.

For a free catalogue listing all available Harlequin Romances,
send your name and address to:

HARLEQUIN READER SERVICE,
M.P.O. Box 707, Niagara Falls, N.Y. 14302
Canadian address: Stratford, Ontario, Canada N5A 6W4

or use coupon at back of books.

# Touched by Fire

by

## JANE DONNELLY

# Harlequin Books

TORONTO • LONDON • NEW YORK • AMSTERDAM • SYDNEY

Original hardcover edition published in 1977
by Mills & Boon Limited

ISBN 0-373-02150-X

Harlequin edition published March 1978

PRINTED IN U.S.A.

# CHAPTER ONE

'I DON'T care if your Uncle Ted does need you,' wailed Fran's mother. 'I need you more.'

Fran Reynolds caught her stepfather's eye over the breakfast table and they exchanged grins. He was a super stepfather, with his patience and his kindness, and this prosperous farm in the Yorkshire dales had been a grand place to grow up in. But Fran loved her uncle too, and his letter read like an appeal for help.

Uncle Ted, her dead father's brother, phoned and wrote regularly. He always came to stay on the farm for Christmas, although he wasn't a countryman in the Yorkshire sense of the word. He developed a hacking cough when the winds were too keen, and he missed his books.

He had been happiest when Fran visited him. Once she had gone down with her mother, and stayed in Edward Reynolds' flat over his shop, but that hadn't been a success. Isabel Martin had wept for Peter Reynolds so that Fran was only thankful that Jim wasn't with them.

Jim Martin had married Isabel Reynolds, a pretty widow, knowing that the great love of her life was her first husband; even though Peter had deserted her and Fran a year before he died. He took her on those terms, he was an easy-going, undemanding man, but it would surely have hurt him to see Isabel walking past the little house where she had once lived with Peter, declaring that that was the only place she had been truly happy.

Fran, fifteen at the time and as fond of Jim as though he had been her real father, had said to Uncle Ted when she and her mother got back from that walk, 'I think I'd better take her home. I don't think this holiday is going to do her much good.'

They had returned to Yorkshire and the farm four days ahead of schedule and Jim had welcomed them back. Jim was a rock, an oak tree. There was all the security any woman could want with Jim and, whatever she said, security was the thing that made Isabel happy.

In Boddington Farm she wanted for nothing, and Jim didn't mind the painting that hung on the living-room wall. Newcomers would look at it and then Isabel would say, 'My first husband painted it. He was Peter Reynolds, the artist.'

Even if they hadn't heard of Peter Reynolds there was such pride in her voice that they often pretended they had. The women at any rate nearly all said, 'Was he really?' and admired the painting.

It was striking, a restless study of hills and storm clouds, showing a talent that might have made his name if he hadn't gone swimming off the coast of Sicily and drowned, just when his pictures were starting to sell. If he had stayed with his wife and daughter he would probably have lived longer, so his bolt for freedom, to paint to his heart's content, had been a tragic mistake.

Fran had missed him desperately when he first went— when she was twelve years old. She had come home from school one day to find her mother distraught, sobbing, 'Your father's gone. He's gone away and left us.'

He had always hated his job as a draughtsman with a local firm. In his spare time he had always painted, and talked of the places he would visit one day, the pictures he would paint. He had gone to find the places, travelling alone, and his brother Ted and Fran had had a grim time with Isabel.

What had hurt Fran most was that he didn't write.

6

She had had a sneaking sympathy for him because, in those days, her mother hadn't had any sympathy at all with his dreams. Fran didn't blame him for going away to find out whether he was a great painter or not. It had seemed romantic to her at first, just like Gauguin, but she hadn't believed then that he was really cutting them out of his life.

They weren't badly off financially. He left them the house and all that was in his bank account. That wasn't much, but he sent a little money every month. But he never wrote a letter nor sent an address.

Isabel grew bitter so that no one dared mention his name, although his brother Edward lived in a state of perpetual apology, always trying to make up to Peter's family for Peter's desertion.

Edward was unmarried himself, and he did his best to be the man about their house, dealing as best he could with each difficulty that arose. He tried to comfort Fran, insisting that her father would return, and at first she believed him. But there were no letters, not even a card when she was thirteen, and two weeks after her birthday Peter Reynolds was beyond return.

When he died Isabel forgave him. Her bitterness dissolved and he was her own dear love again. She was still mourning him when she went on holiday to the Lake District and met Jim, charming him with her soft feminine ways and her air of needing looking after.

Jim Martin was a big man with a big heart. Before the holiday ended he had asked Isabel to marry him, and he travelled home with her to break the news to her daughter and her brother-in-law and her friends.

It was less than six months since Peter had died, and Isabel was not sure how people were going to take this, but although she told everyone that she could never love any other man as much as she had loved Peter she realised how lucky she had been to find Jim.

So did Fran. She liked and trusted him on sight, and Ted was so relieved that Isabel was no longer his responsibility, and that the man she was marrying seemed such a decent fellow, that he didn't realise at first that Isabel's marriage would take Fran away from him.

Ted liked Isabel. He thought Peter had treated her shabbily and he was glad she was getting a second chance at marriage, because she was born to be a wife, just as Edward—and Peter, it seemed—were born bachelors. Isabel could never have managed alone, and Jim Martin would make her a good husband, looking after her and always being there. No danger of Jim ever packing his bags and clearing off.

Ted was fond of Isabel, but Fran was the apple of his eye, and when Isabel and Jim took Fran away to live in the lovely old farmhouse, he felt lost and lonely himself for the first time in his life.

Fran missed her Uncle Ted as much as she had missed her father, but the new life was a good life, and Jim treated her as a daughter during the years she grew from a gangling bright-eyed schoolgirl, with a mop of red hair, into a tall slim young woman who turned heads wherever she went.

The hair was still red, but long and silky. She wasn't as pretty as her mother, but she had an enchanting smile and green eyes with thick dark lashes, and she knew how to use her assets. She brightened up the office of the estate agents where she worked, and the junior partner, who was fairly young, not bad looking and not married, was always asking her out.

That pleased her mother more than it pleased Fran. Fran was twenty-two and her mother was anxious for her to marry and settle down. Fran didn't take life seriously enough for Isabel, because life was serious and finding a nice man was the most important thing of all.

Her mother approved of most of the men Fran brought home, but up to now Fran had had no urge to walk down the aisle with any of them, and certainly not with Arthur Deane, the junior partner, although he was eligible enough if that was what you were after.

Lately Arthur's friendly overtures had become rather more than friendly, and Fran had discussed the problem with Jim, whose advice she valued although they both pretended that her mother was her closest confidante.

Her mother would have told her not to be too hasty, reminding her that one day Arthur would be the senior partner of an old-established family business. 'Don't be so impulsive,' her mother would have said, meaning—this one is a prospective husband and no wanderer, and where are you going to find a steadier man?

Fran's impulsiveness worried her mother. Peter had had the same red hair, and been too impulsive for his own or anyone else's good. More often than not Fran took her emotional tangles to Jim rather than to her mother. Jim was less anxious to see her married, and less bothered about eligibility.

Last Sunday, as they'd walked together over the hills where the sheep and lambs were grazing, she'd said, 'I've got a problem. It's Arthur. He's getting serious.'

'Don't you want him to be serious?' Isabel had drawn Jim's attention to the way Arthur looked at Fran when he brought her back home in the evenings, how anxious he was to let them know that the business was thriving and that he was ready to settle down.

'It won't be long,' Isabel had said happily, 'before he'll be asking you if he can ask Fran to marry him.'

9

Jim had thought he would be well advised to ask Fran first. 'No!' said Fran explosively, and Jim supposed that was the end of that.

'Then what's your problem?' he asked.

'Mother,' said Fran. 'You know how she'll fuss if she finds out.'

Jim chuckled. Indeed he knew. 'Has he asked you to marry him?'

'Not yet, but the signs are there,' said Fran dourly. 'And if he does I might have to leave the office. It could be awkward staying on and jobs aren't two a penny these days, are they?'

It wasn't likely that Fran would be unemployed for long. She had first class secretarial qualifications, but she would be turning in a steady job as well as a steady man, and her mother wouldn't like that at all.

Jim liked it when she asked his advice. 'If it gets that awkward,' he said, 'there's plenty of paper work here to keep you busy until you find something else, and I'll tell your mother I don't think Arthur's right for you. You'll soon find another job.' He looked at the sparkling young face. 'And another lad,' he said.

'Bless you!' Fran flung her arms around him and kissed the weathered cheek soundly. Jim could stand between herself and her mother's exasperation like a solidly built wall. He just smiled and let it all blow over. 'I like my job,' she said, 'if I could just cool it with Arthur.'

Jim chuckled at that, because this stepdaughter of his was not a cool girl. She was gay and generous, open-handed with money and with affection. Arthur was not by any means the first man to fall for her, but he was her employer and since she had begun to make excuses why she shouldn't see him out of working hours he had shown a jealous streak.

He wanted to know exactly where she would be going, what she would be doing, and when the phone rang on Wednesday evening she had been pretty certain it was Arthur, checking up on her.

She had told him she was washing her hair, and so she was. It might be a hackneyed excuse, but it was true, and as there was no one else in the farmhouse at the time she put down her hair dryer and went to answer the phone with a towel around her shoulders.

Her, 'Hello,' was guarded. She hoped he wasn't going to suggest coming round to keep her company.

'Fran?' said Uncle Ted. 'It is Fran, isn't it?'

She began to smile. 'Did I sound very grumpy?'

'You did rather. Is everything all right?'

Her mother and stepfather were out for the evening at friends. She sat down on the old wooden armchair by the phone table in the hall and hugged the phone to her. Dear Uncle Ted! She always enjoyed talking to him. She wished he lived nearer because he was a lovely erudite man, gentle and courtly, full of learning although he lacked Jim's down-to-earth common sense. She had always had a feeling of protectiveness towards Uncle Ted, even in the long-ago days when he was trying so hard to make life easier for herself and her mother.

She said now, laughing to reassure him, 'Boy-friend trouble, I thought that was who was phoning.'

Uncle Ted knew about her boy-friends. She kept in touch, and at Christmas, when he was an honoured guest, they talked and talked together.

'Which one is it this time?' he asked her.

'Arthur Deane. I work for him, and he's getting too serious by half.' It was in recent weeks that Arthur had staked his claim so firmly. She hadn't written or phoned Uncle Ted for a while so this was news to him. 'Trouble is,' she said, 'I can see myself being out of a job, drat the man.'

He sympathised with her, and she told him the rest of the family news. Everyone was well, everything was fine, and how was he?

She had heard him coughing as he talked, and now a paroxysm delayed his answer before he said, 'Not too bad.'

'You're coughing well.'

'Ah yes, that. I'm waiting for the summer. Talking of the summer, have you all fixed your holidays?'

'Mother and Father *are* going to the Canaries.' They had had the travel brochures at Christmas, the holiday discussions had been starting then, the bookings had been made a couple of weeks ago. 'I haven't fixed anything, how about you?' asked Fran. 'How about you coming up here?'

'How about you visiting me?' he said promptly. 'It's nearly three years since you did.'

'Really? That long?' While she was at school and commercial college she had always gone down to Uncle Ted's during her summer holidays. Alone, after the one disastrous time when her mother had accompanied her. She had enjoyed pottering around the flat, helping in the shop, but she supposed it was about three years since her last visit.

'That long,' said Uncle Ted. 'I wish you'd come.'

He had mentioned it at Christmas. He always did, inviting them all, any time. But somehow she got the impression now that he was feeling depressed, and that was why he had rung tonight. She said immediately, 'I'll get a week's holiday just as soon as I can, and I'll come down.'

'You mean that?'

'As soon as I possibly can.'

There was silence for a few seconds. Then Uncle Ted said, 'I'll be waiting for you.'

She almost joked, 'Don't count the days,' but she didn't think he was smiling. She said, 'You take care of yourself. In the morning I'll use up my last bit of influence with Arthur to get my holiday brought forward.'

'Thank you,' he said quietly. 'I'd appreciate that.'

Her mother and Jim were late back, but at breakfast next morning she told them, 'Uncle Ted phoned last night and I've promised to go down for a few days.'

'It should be a nice change for you,' said her mother, pouring tea and watching Fran's breakfast plate. Often as not Fran skipped lunch or settled for a bun in a coffee bar, so Isabel insisted on a cooked breakfast, preparing it herself and putting it down in front of Fran, who would have preferred toast and honey.

'He sounded low,' said Fran, 'and he was coughing badly.'

Her mother smiled tolerantly. 'Ted always was an old woman. Peter used to say he should have been a maiden aunt.'

'Maiden aunts are very trendy these days,' Fran teased. 'They're the ones who've got the best of both worlds.' And her mother frowned, not sure how to deal with that heresy.

Fran fixed her holiday to start in three weeks' time. She explained that her uncle had phoned, and there seemed no reason why she shouldn't go. Business wasn't that brisk.

Arthur knew about Uncle Ted. Everyone who knew

13

Fran did, the two men had met last Christmas, but for all that Fran got an old-fashioned look from Arthur when she asked for some of her holiday leave right away to visit her uncle.

'That's where you were born, isn't it?' said Arthur. 'Do you still have plenty of friends down there?'

'Not many,' she said. 'It's years since I was there, and then it was only for a few days.'

'No loyal old sweethearts?' smiled Arthur.

'No, worse luck,' said Fran lightly.

She resented this prying, although it was ridiculous. She might have said, 'I don't have a lover in those parts. There's a nice man who works in the galleries next to the crafts shop, and there's also the only man I've ever really detested. There's always the risk of meeting him when I go visiting Uncle Ted.'

But she wasn't close enough to Arthur to be telling him things like that, and she never spoke about Leon Aldridge to anyone if she could possibly help it.

She wrote to Uncle Ted that day, with her date of arrival, and their letters crossed. His came with next morning's mail and she scanned it quickly, then bit her lip and started again, reading slowly, weighing up all the implications.

If you weren't familiar with the crabbed handwriting it took some reading, but Fran knew this writing nearly as well as her own.

'Since I spoke to you on the telephone,' Uncle Ted wrote, 'I've been thinking over what you told me about the possibility of your leaving your job. I presume you have nothing else in mind, and I wonder if you would consider coming here and helping me. These days I'm feeling my age.'

He was quite a bit older than her father, but he must

still only be in his fifties. She read on with a growing conviction that this was not just a suggestion to deal with her problem. She knew that Uncle Ted would have welcomed her any time, but this letter seemed to say more than appeared on the surface.

Her mother was at the stove, presiding over a pan of frying eggs. Jim sat at the table, opening his mail, and Fran pushed the letter across to him. 'Read this,' she said.

Her mother turned at that to ask, 'What is it?' but Fran didn't answer immediately. She waited until Jim looked up from the letter, then she said,

'Uncle Ted's suggesting I go and stay down there and help him run the craft shop.'

'What?' The egg slipped from the scoop back into the pan, and while she was retrieving it Isabel gave a snort of derision. 'What a stupid idea! He must be going senile.'

'I think he needs me,' said Fran quietly.

Her mother put the egg on the plate and the plate in front of Fran and said, 'I don't care if your Uncle Ted does need you, I need you more.'

Fran and Jim smiled wryly at each other, and Isabel knew they were laughing at her a little. She said shrilly, 'You've got a job here. You've got Arthur here.'

She had to be told if Fran was going to take up this offer, and Fran said, 'Sorry, Mother, but I don't want Arthur, and if I turn Arthur down I think I'll have talked myself out of the job.'

It was too much for Isabel, so early in the morning. She sat down in her chair at the table and slumped back croaking, 'Jim, tell her, stop her!'

Jim said mildly, 'She wouldn't be emigrating.'

'Give me the letter.' Isabel leaned forward and took it, blinking and peering because she had no patience with illegible handwriting. It was short enough, and she said snappishly, 'If he needs an assistant I'm sure he can find one.'

Fran said, 'It's a funny letter.'

Isabel tossed it down again on the table. 'It doesn't make me laugh.'

'I mean it's odd.' Her mother had known what she meant. Fran hunched her shoulders. 'I can't explain it, but I feel I ought to be reading something between the lines.'

She looked appealingly at Jim; her mother had no sympathy for any message that hadn't been plainly spelled out. Jim was stolid and unimaginative, but he was very practical and he suggested, 'You could go down for a month and see how you go on.'

It was such a temptation to get away from Arthur that that might be why she was telling herself that Uncle Ted needed her so badly. But if he did a month would show it, and it would be fun to give a hand in the shop. She had always worked in offices, but perhaps the time had come for a change. She said, 'I could do that, couldn't I? I could hand in my notice this morning,' and her mother shrieked at her,

'No! Oh, you're so impulsive, you never stop to *think*.' She banged the table with her clenched fists, her face crumpling like a child's. 'Now you've decided to walk out and leave me too,' she wailed. 'Just like your father did.'

That wasn't true. Fran had been a deeply caring daughter and still was.

'Steady on, now,' Jim began, and Isabel turned on him. 'You don't understand, how can you? I don't want Fran going away, working in Ted's shop. I hate that

16

shop, next to the galleries and that terrible man. I couldn't even go to see her there.'

'Steady on, old girl,' said Jim, and Fran recognised his little signal that she should get out and leave this to him. She jumped up and her mother said automatically,

'You're not going to work without your breakfast.'

'Plenty of time for that,' said Jim, although Fran never gave herself any time to spare in the mornings.

She stood outside the kitchen door for a few minutes. She heard her mother's high-pitched voice, but it was a stout door and Jim's deep voice didn't reach her. She would have to put her ear to the wood to get the drift of the argument, and eavesdropping seemed rather mean, even though she was the one under discussion.

There wouldn't be a row going on. They never rowed, because Jim never argued; not like the old arguments in the old days between her mother and her father. Jim was always good-tempered, but this was taking time, and Fran took her camel coat off the hallstand, collected her tan-coloured handbag from the living room, and went across to the garage.

She drove her car out and sat in it, watching the house and waiting. She didn't want to be late for work. If she was handing in her notice that would be rather adding insult to injury. But she had to hang around until Jim came out and told her whether her mother was reconciled to her leaving or not.

Suppose she wasn't? Suppose she carried on like she'd done when Fran's father had left them? She'd just said, 'You've decided to walk out and leave me, like your father did,' and Fran could remember how dreadful the days that followed that desertion had been.

Uncle Ted had been wonderful then, and now of course there was Jim. He'd tell her that she wasn't losing

Fran, that there was no comparison at all. Fran also hoped he would tell her to count her blessings.

She turned on the little radio she usually carried in her car, and listened to music and time signals and bright D.J. chatter, until she saw the back door open and Jim come out into the yard. Then she wound down the window and called as he walked towards her, 'How is she?'

He was grinning. 'Ah, she'll be all right,' he said. His eyes were kind and tenderly amused. 'It came as a shock to her, she thought things were coming on nicely between you and Arthur Deane. Do you want to go and work for your Uncle Ted?'

'Yes, I think I do.' She would miss Jim, and her mother of course, and the farm. She said, 'Like you say, I can go down there for a holiday and see how it works out.' She pulled a face. 'I don't know why Mother's making such a fuss. She'd be thrilled to pieces if I got married and moved out.'

'But you'd be settled then, wouldn't you?' said Jim sagely. 'She'd know where she could find you and it wouldn't be more than a few miles away.' Isabel was watching them through the kitchen window, and Jim said quietly, 'She's never forgotten that your father walked out. That's why she's so possessive about you.'

She was possessive and she had been hurt, but ever since she had married Jim she had been cherished, and Fran said hotly, 'She's probably had a darn sight better life here than she'd have had if he'd stayed and she'd never met you.'

She wasn't concerned at the moment whether it was true, but her stepfather had always done his best for both of them and she was grateful; and she knew that her mother was, although she couldn't let the memory of her first husband die.

'You're a good lass,' said Jim.

And he was a good man. 'You'll take care of her, won't you?'

'Don't I always?' He took his pipe out of his pocket, he looked right with a pipe, puffing contentedly. 'And she takes care of me,' he said.

'Of course,' said Fran. Her mother loved this attractive old house, the money to be comfortable and buy pretty things. She loved fussing over Jim and Fran, preparing attractive meals, having her friends round for coffee. She was not made for hard times and Fran was leaving her in good hands.

Jim stood back as she started up the car. 'Now I've got to break the news to Arthur,' she said as she went, and she left him chuckling.

This was the town she knew best of all. She had finished her education here, gone through a couple of earlier office jobs before moving on to Arthur's firm twelve months ago, and she had always been happy. There had been little miseries, of course, little downs, but on the whole she had been very happy, and she could have stayed here and made this the centre of her life for the rest of her life.

But she had welcomed the chance of escape in Uncle Ted's letter. She needed a change, although explaining that to Arthur might be tricky.

The estate agents had attractive bow-fronted windows, and a big light reception room, with an artificial flower arrangement in an alcove; and Mrs Lowndes, who had been here for thirty years, behind the counter.

She and Fran said good morning to each other as Fran hurried through the door behind the counter that led to

Arthur's office. Fran's desk was in here, and so was Arthur, because she was ten minutes late and he was always punctual.

He glanced at his watch as she hung up her coat, but made no comment about the time. He was surprised, that was all, she was usually here on the dot too. He expected her to say that her car had given trouble, or explain what had held her up.

She sat down at her desk and he was still looking inquiringly at her when she turned to face him.

Arthur was plump and smooth, and would grow plumper and smoother with the years. Fran could see why her mother fancied him for her. He wasn't built for running away.

She was a little nervous about the scene that was coming, and she took off the cover of her typewriter and fiddled with things on her desk as she told him, 'I had a letter from Uncle Ted this morning.'

'The one you're going to stay with?'

'I've only got one uncle.' He knew she had, but she need not have snapped even if she was nervous, and she said quickly, 'Yes, that one. Well, he wants me to stay and help him run the shop.'

'Stay?' Arthur's shiny receding brow crinkled. 'How long?'

'Er—permanently.' Whatever happened she wouldn't be coming back to work here.

'But you're not a saleswoman.' He sounded as though this must have been overlooked and someone should point it out.

'I can learn,' said Fran.

'But you're a secretary.'

'There'll be letters and ledgers down there.'

The news was sinking in. After a moment or two he

said, 'I'll never be able to replace you.' She presumed he was talking about work, he was looking worriedly at his 'In' tray and she said reassuringly,

'Of course you will. I'll get all the files and correspondence up to date and you'll advertise and——'

'But what about *us*?' He pushed back his chair and stood up, the colour rising in his smooth skin, stammering a little. 'I thought we—you know how I feel about you——' He gulped and got out a complete sentence, 'If you're going away I think we should make it official.'

He hadn't actually asked her to marry him before, but he had brought up the subject more than once. He probably believed they had an understanding, although Fran had always avoided an outright declaration.

She stood up too. 'Don't let's be hasty,' she said. 'I don't think this is the time to come to any decisions about anything.'

He came from behind his desk. 'Fran——' he began, and she kept her desk between them, moving round so that she was well out of his reach. He could hardly chase her round it, if he did she was quicker on her feet than he was, but she didn't want to bruise his ego.

She said, 'We're very good friends, aren't we? Let's keep it that way, shall we?' and he stopped circling the desk. He looked at her and sighed, and then went back to his chair, sat down in it heavily and sighed again.

'You're determined about this?' he asked her.

'Yes, I am.'

'He wants you to go down there, does he?'

She sat down too. 'Yes, he says he's feeling his age.' She prattled on, 'It's a smashing little shop. Everything in it is made by local craftsmen. There's something of everything: carving, metal work, things made of glass, pottery, even toys. There are handwoven skirts and scarves and cloaks. Not paintings, but everything else.'

Her father had sold some of his early pictures in the crafts shop, but Uncle Ted wasn't an art dealer.

'And you're all the family he's got?' Arthur was asking.

'Yes.' She offered an explanation that she hoped he might accept. 'I have to go. There's really no one else he can call on.'

'So it'll come to you eventually,' said Arthur, and Fran stared at him.

'You mean I'll inherit it?' She had never thought about that. Please God, that was twenty or thirty years away.

'So I suppose you want to help keep the business to-gether.' He looked at the door as though he was checking it was still shut, then leaned forward, speaking softly and confidentially. 'As a business man may I give you some advice?'

She wondered what an estate agent would know about running a crafts shop, but she said, 'Please do.'

'I'd stay with the farm if I were you.' He gave her a cagey little nod. 'I'm not saying that Mr Martin would ever turn against you, but you are only his stepdaughter. As long as you're here you're the one he'll leave it to, but if you go away there's always the chance——'

Fran couldn't help it. Laughter was bubbling up in her, and her voice shook with suppressed giggles. 'You are planning ahead, aren't you? You've just killed off every living relative I've got!' The pink in his face turned pinker with embarrassment, and she told him, 'I reckon my stepfather will outlive you, and my mother wouldn't be flattered to hear you think she's got one foot in the grave.'

He began to bluster, 'I never said anything of the sort.' But it seemed that one of her charms for Arthur Deane was the fact that she was the stepdaughter of a prosperous farmer.

She said, 'I do like a practical man, but this is ridiculous.'

She wasn't hurt, because she had never for a moment thought she was in love with Arthur. She had enough self-confidence to find this funny. The cheek of the man! The mercenary little prig.

I should worry about you, she thought. 'A week's notice, then,' she said.

She didn't tell her mother why Arthur felt she should be staying here, her mother would not have been amused, but she told Jim when she got him alone for a few minutes that evening. Her mother was on the telephone in the hall, talking to one of her friends, and Fran said, 'Arthur thinks I'm a heiress, but if I leave here you'll cut me off. It's the farm he's after, not me.'

Jim chuckled. 'I don't suppose he'd mind the farm, but it's you he fancies. He very likely thinks he's looking after your interests. You could tell him you'll get the farm some day, for what it's worth, but I'll probably outlast him.'

'That's what I did tell him.' Through the not-quite closed door she heard the phone jingle as her mother put down the receiver, and finished quickly, 'That you're going to live longer than he is, so see you do or you'll make me out a liar!'

Isabel's friend had been commiserating with her on Fran leaving home, and Isabel came back into the room to say again what she had been saying all evening: 'How can you possibly move out in a *week*?'

'I could pack all I shall need in fifteen minutes,' said Fran. 'I could be back here in a matter of hours for anything I've forgotten.'

But the move wasn't quite as easy or as simple as that. She wasn't going far, nor to strangers, but it was still an uprooting. Her way of life would be changed. She would have to make new friends and compared to the solid comfort and security of family life in the old farmhouse she would be out on her own.

She spent most of the week saying goodbyes, and the days flew by. Her mother had now decided that this was a holiday and nothing more, but somehow Fran didn't think so. She felt she was making a real break, although she could get back here without any trouble, any time.

Her mother waved her goodbye, calling, 'Phone us as soon as you arrive, and we'll see you in four weeks. Have a lovely time.'

It was a pleasant drive, and a straightforward route, although it was three years since Fran had taken it. She had been nineteen then; her little second-hand car, a birthday present from Jim and her mother, was still going strong today and she hoped it would stay good for another year or two.

She was looking forward to seeing Uncle Ted, his shop had always been something of a treasure trove in her mind. Although she hadn't inherited her father's artistic talents of course she loved beautiful things, and working among them should be more rewarding than tapping away indefinitely on a typewriter.

She had no fear of loneliness, she had always been able to make friends, and as the music played on the little radio on the seat beside her she hummed the tunes, and the sun was shining and everything looked bright.

She had probably exaggerated that uneasy feeling that

Uncle Ted's letter had given her. When she'd phoned and told him she was coming he had sounded delighted, no longer depressed, and why should there be anything the matter? She was getting fanciful.

She reached Stratford-upon-Avon around four o'clock in the afternoon. It was market day in town, the centre of the square was filled with stalls and the traffic edged slowly round. Next Friday she would be able to come shopping here, and she scanned the faces of pedestrians, not expecting to recognise anybody—at least three-quarters were tourists—but she might see someone she had met on earlier visits to Uncle Ted, or even someone she had known when she lived here.

Uncle Ted's shop had one of the best positions in town. It was a small part of a rather spectacular black and white Elizabethan house, set back from the road by a flag-stoned forecourt. The downstairs windows were no longer leaded, but clear now for display purposes. In the biggest windows paintings, and an occasional small piece of sculpture were shown, and the name on the windows was 'Aldridge Galleries'.

The crafts shop was at the far end. In front of it were roughly hewn tables and chairs, garden furniture, in natural wood. The crafts shop had always looked cheap and cheerful compared to the galleries. Customers entered by a side door instead of the impressive central door that led into the galleries. Parking was through an archway this side of the house as Fran turned off the road.

As she did a tall man came out of the gallery, and stood looking at her car, then at her. He was wearing beige trousers and a blue denim shirt, casual wear, but he was arrogantly elegant. His straight fair hair flopped a little over his eyes, and his eyes she remembered were

Arctic blue. She had never seen eyes colder than his remembered eyes.

They faced each other, with no sign of recognition, then Fran jerked round and fumbled a gear change, furious with herself. She got the car through the archway and drove to the far end of the courtyard where Uncle Ted's old Austin Cambridge was parked.

When she switched off she sat for a moment, her stomach churning as though she had stepped into a lift that had dropped too fast.

He hadn't changed. She had seen him the last time she was here, briefly of course, accidentally. He must have recognised her now, but she hadn't expected him to acknowledge her. They never had had anything to say to each other.

She shuddered. Leon Aldridge, waiting for her. No, of course he wasn't waiting for her. It was coincidence that he had walked out of the door as she turned into the forecourt. But there he was, even before she'd got out of her car and set foot on what was going to be her home territory. If she had been superstitious this would surely have been a black omen.

# CHAPTER TWO

THERE were no customers in the crafts shop when Fran went in by the side door, to the faint tinkle of the bell, and Uncle Ted came out of the office. He was a tallish ascetic-looking man with a slight stoop, and the joy in his voice when he said her name made her drop her case and run to him, hugging him close.

'Am I glad to see you!' she said.

'You came.' He held her at arm's length, looking at her. 'Even after you rang and said you'd be here I could still hardly believe it.'

'Oh, I'm real enough.' She hoped it was the muted lighting of the shop that was making him look haggard. 'You're thin,' she said accusingly.

'Of course I'm thin.' He had a nice lopsided grin. 'I've always been thin.'

Yes, he had. Perhaps she was comparing him with her stepfather, who was built on a much heftier frame. All the same she said, 'Do you get enough to eat?' then laughed, 'I sound like my mother!'

Uncle Ted collected her case, as she walked up the stairs to the landing of the little flat ahead of him. 'I thought your mother might stop you coming,' he said.

'She wasn't enthusiastic,' Fran admitted. 'I must phone them tonight. Oh, this is nice. Is it really three years since I was here?'

The living room was comfortable, with rather dilapidated furniture. Two old wickerwork armchairs were one each side of the fireplace, exactly as they had been as long as she remembered. The ceiling was beamed, the wooden floor was covered with rugs, and there was a lot of clutter about. 'Will you mind if I tidy up a little?' she said. 'If there are going to be two of us in here.'

He put down her case and swept out his arms. 'You can sweep it all out of the door if you like. You can do anything you like with it so long as you stay.'

'I wouldn't dream of anything so drastic.' She sat down and bounced on the sofa. 'It's good lived-in stuff, is this. I used to jump up and down on this when I was a baby, didn't I?'

'You were an energetic child.' He smiled nostalgically and the shop's doorbell rang again below. 'You know your room, don't you?'

She should know it. It was off the same landing as the living rooms. Uncle Ted's bedroom and a storeroom were up another flight of stairs, under the eaves.

She took her case into her room while he went down into the shop. It had always been a pleasant little room, with white walls and light wood furniture, but today it smelt of fresh paint. The walls were pale green and there was a vase of daffodils on the chest of drawers.

Uncle Ted had worked hard to pretty her room. The kitchen-cum-diner had a savoury aroma, and he had laid the table for two. When she opened the oven door there was a casserole inside. Everything had been prepared to welcome her, and she went down into the shop as the customers left. 'I love my room,' she said, 'and the flowers.'

He looked pleased. 'Good sale?' she asked, as the door closed behind the customers.

'Every little helps.'

'You'll have to show me around the stock.' She picked up a pink glass paperweight with a price ticket on the bottom. 'Is everything marked?'

'Most of them. I think I'll close early tonight. You

probably want to have a wash after your journey, and the food should be about ready, so I'll see you upstairs in about ten minutes.'

She washed hands and face, put back a light dash of make-up, and when she took the casserole out of the oven and lifted the lid she found that it was cooked to a turn. Casseroled pork chops, smelling of herbs, mushrooms, and onions, and baked potatoes in their jackets on another tray.

She served them both and they sat down to eat. As she tasted she said, 'You're still a good cook, and I was wrong about you not having enough to eat.'

'I didn't bother much when I was on my own.' He was eating with an appetite now, beaming and contented, and Fran realised just how lonely he must have been.

She had never thought of him as lonely. He had always lived alone. He had bought this shop when he was a young man and he had always been here. But perhaps the passing years and his not-too-robust health had taken the gilt off solitude.

He was so glad to have her here and she chattered about things that she thought would interest or amuse him, including Arthur's suggestion that she might lose the farm if she didn't stay put. 'How about that for keeping an eye on the main chance?' she grinned, 'and I thought it was me he was crazy about!'

Uncle Ted didn't smile until he was sure there was no hurt in Fran's smile, then he did. He was smiling when she said, 'That's put me off men for a bit. And talking about men I can do without, guess whose was the first familiar face I saw when I arrived this afternoon.' Uncle Ted shook his head. 'Leon Aldridge.' She said that as though it was the name of a mass murderer, with an exaggerated grimace of distaste. 'Yeuk! Is he here much?'

There were Aldridge Galleries in London, New York and Rome, but this was where the Aldridge home was, a couple of miles down the river on an island all its own.

Uncle Ted had stopped smiling. He said quietly, 'He's away next week.'

'That's someting,' said Fran cheerfully. 'Just as I was driving in he came out. Why him now? Why not a customer or one of the staff? I crossed my fingers in case it was a bad luck sign.'

'Did you speak to him?'

'You're joking!' She had had a mushroom on her fork for quite a while. She ate it, then asked, 'What would I say? Long time no see—but not long enough?'

She had thought they were joking, he usually smiled about her dislike for Leon Aldridge, but now he said quite seriously, 'I know how you feel about him, but he will be around.'

If she was going to live here they were bound to meet, but of course she wouldn't antagonise a neighbour. She could never like him, but she would be civil. She began to promise that, when there was a rat-tat on the door on the landing.

Once this building had been a house. Two doors connected the crafts shop and flat with the larger premises of the gallery. One door down in the shop, a second on the landing. They were bolted and barred on both sides, the one downstairs had a big display cabinet in front of it, and this was the first time Fran had ever heard anyone knock from the gallery. She hadn't thought that door was ever used.

She tried to laugh, 'Don't tell me he's followed me!'

still joking but with an uncomfortable stiffening of all her muscles.

Uncle Ted got up and went out of the living room along the landing. Fran heard bolts being drawn back, then she heard him say, 'Hello, Gerald, come on through,' and she relaxed.

Gerald would be Gerald Maddox who managed the galleries. She jumped up, very glad to see him because he wasn't Leon Aldridge, and also because when she was last here three years ago he was the nice young man with whom she went round to a pub for a drink one night, and to the cinema on another evening.

When she went home she had promised to come back during her next holiday. He phoned her a couple of times in the following six months, and for about the same length of time they had passed friendly messages through Uncle Ted. It was still occasionally, 'Remember me to Gerald,' or Fran, but he was rather a dim memory to Fran as she was sure she was to him.

All the same, she was pleased to see him. She said, 'How lovely, and don't you look well?'

He was in his late twenties, with a dark moustache and twinkling eyes behind horn-rimmed spectacles. He wore a conservative navy blue suit, and looked like the manager of a high class establishment, but Fran remembered he had had a sense of humour, and been less stuffy than he looked.

He looked at her now and then grinned at Uncle Ted. 'This should be good for trade.'

'I hope so,' smiled Uncle Ted. 'Cup of tea?'

'Thanks.'

'I'll get it,' said Fran.

They had almost finished the casserole and there was none left over, so while she waited for the kettle to boil she found cheese and biscuits, put them on a tray and took them into the living room. 'Now,' she said, putting the tray on the table and speaking to Gerald, 'tell me all your news.'

'I'm still next door.' Still working next door, he meant. 'And how is it you're not married?' he asked her.

'I take after my uncle, I'm hard to catch.' She poured tea for Uncle Ted, scooping in the sugar, then asked Gerald, 'Milk? Sugar?'

'Milk, no sugar, please.'

As she handed him the cup she said, 'Anyhow, look who's talking. Why aren't you married? Or are you?' Uncle Ted might have forgotten to pass on the news. He wouldn't have thought it that important. Nor was it, to Fran. If Gerald was married she wished him happiness and she would like to meet his wife.

'Not yet,' he said, with such flirtatious meaning that she burst out laughing.

They sat before the fire, talking. He seemed in no hurry to get home. He had the ground floor of a small terraced house in town, she remembered, the same type she had lived in before her mother married Jim, and he made himself comfortably at home now, drinking tea until the pot ran dry.

He was still fired with enthusiasm for his job. He talked about that at length. Next month they were putting on an exhibition for a new painter. 'Leon found her,' he said, and Fran muttered,

'A great talent-spotter.'

'Yes, indeed,' said Gerald.

Uncle Ted shifted in his seat, reaching towards the television. 'You won't mind if I listen to the news, will you?'

'Is that the time?' Gerald checked his watch in astonishment. 'I never realised. I only looked in to say it will be nice having you here.'

He sounded as guilty as though he had outstayed his welcome. He hadn't so far as Fran was concerned, although she suspected that Uncle Ted hadn't wanted her disparaging Leon Aldridge to his manager. She doubted if she would have done. She hadn't gone into details three years ago, if Gerald remembered the only thing she had said about Leon was that he wasn't her type. Nor would she now, but Uncle Ted seemed more sensitive than he used to be about Leon Aldridge.

'See you tomorrow, maybe?' Gerald said to her.

'I'll be here,' she said. 'Which way out? Through the connecting door or through our side door?'

He shrugged. 'It doesn't matter. I locked up before I came through, I don't have to go back into the gallery.'

He went down the stairs into the crafts shop and Fran walked down with him, opening the side door for him. 'Just like old times,' he said, and that made her smile because all they had shared were two very innocuous evenings. They had no old times.

'I think you're thinking of two other folk,' she said, and went upstairs still smiling.

Uncle Ted was listening to the news, which soon took her smile away. It wasn't often there was much to smile at in the news. She carried the cups and saucers to the sink and washed them, and came back and sat on a hassock by the fire, watching the glow and wondering what time was bedtime for Uncle Ted. Three years ago it had been around eleven o'clock on a working day, but he looked wearier now.

As the news ended he turned down the sound so that it wasn't much more than a murmuring background. 'About Leon——' he began.

'Oh dear, must we?' Fran didn't want to discuss the man. He had obtruded quite enough on her first evening here.

'It was a long time ago,' said Uncle Ted quietly. 'You shouldn't blame him.'

'You know I don't.' He *was* looking careworn. He hadn't been too robust at Christmas, but that had been winter, now it was spring, and he still looked as though he was carrying a heavy load. If he was concerned that she might cause trouble she must reassure him. She said, 'My father would have cleared off even if he'd never met Leon Aldridge. You know he couldn't paint at home.'

Uncle Ted nodded silently.

Although she had long forgotten that herself, Isabel had looked on Peter Reynolds' art as a threat to the monthly pay cheque and the secure life. But Uncle Ted and Fran remembered. They knew that Peter would probably have gone one day, even without Leon Aldridge's advice—to get away and paint.

That was what any expert who disliked seeing talent smothered might have said, and fair enough. Her mother blamed Leon Aldridge. Her mother had blamed everyone but herself. Sometimes in the early days, even Uncle Ted and Fran. She said Edward had lent Peter money—although Uncle Ted had never had any money to lend anyone—and Fran had encouraged her father by liking his work. That was part of the dreadful months. She hadn't said anything like that since Peter died, but she would always blame Leon Aldridge.

Fran didn't blame him. He had been twenty-four when her father left home, but he was already a name in the art world. The Aldridge Galleries, under his grandfather and father, had been dignified emporiums, dealing only with established artists, most of them dead. But Leon

34

began his career as an art dealer, buying the work of young painters and sculptors. When he promoted anyone it was an accolade for the artist because, from the beginning, his judgment had rarely been faulted. Having asked for Leon Aldridge's verdict on his work Peter Reynolds had acted on it.

Fran blamed no one for that. But Aldridge had also stressed that an artist must be ruthless, and Peter Reynolds had made a ruthless break. No letters, no birthday card.

Fran hadn't known Leon Aldridge in those days. He wasn't at these galleries a great deal, his father was alive then and permanently in the home-town galleries. Leon was the jet-man, the cosmopolitan. Fran saw him occasionally, but they had never spoken. The young tycoon probably never even noticed the schoolgirl who came to the crafts shop. If she saw him he made no impact on her. He was Leon Aldridge, so what?

Then her father packed his paints and a small suitcase and walked out of their lives, and the man who had called ruthlessness a virtue came into focus for Fran.

Next time she saw him she looked hard at him. He didn't know she was watching. She saw him through the crafts shop window. She was minding the store while her Uncle Ted was round at their house, going through papers, that her father had always handled, with her mother.

Leon Aldridge came out of the galleries and stood talking with another man. Fran knew his features, now for the first time she saw that he had blue eyes, blue as the heart of an iceberg, that he talked without smiling. He was tall and still, without gestures or any wasted effort, and she shivered because he looked so cold, so self-contained.

He could still make her shiver. Seeing him when she'd turned her car this afternoon had sent ice into her veins. She used to call him the Iceman, to Uncle Ted. She never called him anything to her mother, because in those early days the mention of Leon Aldridge was enough to send Isabel into hysterics. There was one scene when Isabel had stormed into the galleries, and then Uncle Ted had lost his temper with her and she'd shut herself in her bedroom for hours.

'She can't blame Leon Aldridge,' Uncle Ted had told the twelve-year-old Fran that day. 'If your father's going to do anything worth while he has to get away. He'll be back.'

'I know he will.' Fran had believed it then.

Now she said, 'It's just that I'm not fond of icemen. I've got this funny feeling that if you get too near one you're asking for frostbite.'

Uncle Ted protested, 'You don't know him,' and she agreed.

'No, I don't, I'm just prejudiced, I don't really want to know him.' As Uncle Ted still looked worried she asked, 'Do I have to?'

'Well,' his smile was wintry as though he could offer little comfort, 'as I said before, he is around more these days, and he's not a man I want to offend.'

'But I'm not going to offend him.' She was a peace-loving girl to whom aggro had never appealed, although she did tend to find herself where the sparks were flying. She hoped she was here to make Uncle Ted's life easier and she said gaily, 'I can't see him bothering me and I promise you I won't bother him.'

Her uncle laughed at that, and they spent the rest of the evening quietly and comfortably. Fran phoned her mother, then she and her uncle settled down for an hour or two with a book each, and Leon Aldridge's name didn't come up again.

She had expected to fall asleep as soon as her head touched the pillow, she usually did. But tonight different surroundings and the prospect of a different tomorrow combined to keep her mind active. After she had tossed and turned for over an hour she realised that her throat was dry and she could use a glass of milk.

There was plenty in the fridge. If she got up and warmed some it might lull her to sleep. She could pull the bedroom curtains across the window at the same time, because moonlight was flooding the room so that it was nearly as bright as day.

She didn't need to switch on the light. The landing was quiet and empty. Upstairs Uncle Ted was almost certainly sleeping the sleep of the just. Fran's bedroom was at the end of the passage so that she stepped out by the connecting door into the gallery. It was still unbolted, and she went to secure it—automatically, not because she expected anything to be coming through.

She had no excuse for what happened next, except that she was born inquisitive. She had never been inside the Galleries, although they had been next door to the crafts shop long before she was born, and she couldn't resist this opportunity for a quick and private peek. She opened the door and looked through.

The small rooms of the upper floors had been opened up, supported by timbers. The landing was an upper gallery, with a carved balustrade and an imposing staircase. This was the main part of the house, of course. The crafts shop and the flat were very unimpressive compared with this, and she tiptoed a little way in, enjoying herself like a Victorian child peeping down at an adult dinner party.

It was light enough to see pictures, on walls, on easels; and sculpture, ranging from tiny pieces in cabinets to a massive creation down below. She might ask Gerald how much they were asking for that, and who on earth would be likely to buy it.

Suddenly she tensed. She had been gazing aimlessly around when she saw one small canvas on the wall, a little farther along, in the same style as her father's work. She went slowly towards it. If it was it was an old picture, there was no doubt at all that her father had drowned. He had been brought from the sea within minutes and identified with no possibility of error. But this could be something he had painted during those twelve months.

It wasn't. She couldn't quite make out the signature, but she could read last year's date, and when she stood closer the similarity was slight. Another artist did bold brush strokes, that was really all it amounted to.

She walked back, towards the connecting door, looking at the wall and the paintings, and somehow brushing against a pedestal that was beside the gallery rail.

It might have swayed back if she had reacted less violently. But as her shoulder touched she whirled round, trying frantically to counteract her clumsiness and making matters infinitely worse. She didn't catch the vase that was teetering, but she did knock it over the rail, down on to the floor below.

She daren't look. She had heard the smash, high and thin and delicate like distant sleigh bells, or the breaking of exquisite expensive china.

She ran down the stairs, gulping dry sobs of panic, and went on to her knees at the point of contact. The vase was in so many pieces there was no chance of repair—if indeed that kind of thing could ever be repaired, and offered at a 'knock-down' price.

She clapped her hand to her mouth. 'Knock-down price' indeed! This was no laughing matter. Not only was she trespassing but she had just destroyed a very valuable item for which she was morally and legally responsible.

She picked up the largest piece. The design on it looked like the scales of a dragon. Chinese? Ming? One of those fabulous dynasties that were priced in thousands?

However much it was, she owed for it, and she would have to explain to Gerald and find out how much, and then start working out how to get the money together. She would have to phone home. 'Hello. Yes, I'm fine, thanks, do you think you could let me have a couple of thousand pounds as soon as possible, I've just dropped a Ming vase?'

Please don't let it be too valuable. Let it be something she could pay for, even if she had to sell her little car to do it.

She was gathering up the pieces by the light of the moon. They glimmered pale as eggshells on the dark floor, and if she left them scattered all around whoever opened up the Galleries in the morning would think there had been a break-in and probably phone the police. She would have to get whoever came in first and explain and she prayed it would be Gerald.

Perhaps she would phone him at home. She could do that now. It would be easier to confess over the phone, and if she felt like fainting when he told her the price she wouldn't have far to stagger to bed.

She had her hands full with the pieces—it had been a big vase. She went upstairs and put the pieces down by the pedestal, then went back through the door again into

Uncle Ted's cosy little flat, wishing with all her heart that she had never left it.

This was a fine start. Poor Uncle Ted, who was so anxious that she shouldn't get on the wrong side of Leon Aldridge. If he knew what she had been up to these last five minutes he'd be having nightmares up there.

She was so shaken that it took her a while to remember Gerald's surname. She sat in the little office behind the crafts shop, where the telephone was, with a phone directory on her knee, going through the C's because that seemed the right initial. When 'Maddox' came to her she started again, but she couldn't find one that had a likely address, and she shut the directory with a sigh.

She would have to wait till morning. She dragged herself up to bed, and when she did fall asleep she dreamt of Chinese dragons. But instead of breathing fire they breathed ice, and her first thought when she woke was—however much do I owe Leon Aldridge?

There was no call to worry Uncle Ted until she had to, so she put on the kettle and laid the table for breakfast. And every few minutes after eight o'clock she ran down-stairs, and out through the side door to the front of the building to see if the Galleries were open.

Uncle Ted, in pyjamas and an old maroon-coloured dressing gown, came down at twenty past eight, pleased to see her up and about and pink-cheeked. 'Did you sleep well?' he inquired.

'Yes,' she fibbed. 'Did you?'

'Best night's sleep I've had in months,' he said.

Oh dear, she thought, oh *dear*! As he went into the bathroom she rushed down the stairs again, out through the side door of the crafts shop, and this time the door of the gallery opened when she tried it.

She went in and Leon Aldridge came to meet her. He

wasn't in a denim shirt today. He was in a slate grey suit, impeccably tailored, grey shirt and grey tie. His features would have been classically regular if his nose had not been broken some time. Not badly, she supposed some women might think it made him look interesting. But he was the last man she ever wanted to see, especially now.

She said breathlessly, 'I was looking for Gerald.'

'He should be in shortly.'

Fran felt she was cringing, that she would creep out like Uriah Heep, but she couldn't tell Leon Aldridge what had brought her here. Uncle Ted had said he was away next week. If she could settle with Gerald, if she could pay for the vase, perhaps Leon Aldridge need never know that she had broken it.

'Would it be anything to do with the vase?' he asked, and then she saw the pieces she had missed. There were several still lying about. 'I noticed the door was un-barred,' he said.

Her mind ticked over at panic rate. He'd seen the pieces. He'd gone up and found the rest, obviously placed there, and he'd noticed the door unbarred. There was no way round this except open confession, and how could she word it so that Gerald didn't get part of the blame?

She croaked, trying for time to think, 'You know who I am?'

'Of course.' She wouldn't have been surprised if he hadn't. In other circumstances she might have said, 'If you recognised me yesterday why did you look through me?' But in these circumstances she said meekly,

'I'm terribly sorry. It was me. I looked in, you see.' She pointed towards the door upstairs, although there was no need, he knew how she had entered his premises. 'And I saw a painting that reminded me of my father's work—I thought it might have been one of his.' She paused. When he said nothing she said, 'Peter Reynolds.'

He could hardly have forgotten, although it was ten years ago. 'We did sell his paintings,' he said, 'but there were very few of them.'

'He didn't have much time, did he?'

'Unfortunately no.' That sounded more like an official pronouncement than genuine sympathy. 'They haven't come on the market again,' he said, so they were talking about the paintings, not the man.

But it meant that the buyers must have been happy with their pictures, and she asked, 'Were they good? Would he have been a great artist?'

'He had talent but, as you say, not enough time.'

'So it was a pity he didn't stay where he was, at home,' Fran said impulsively.

'Possibly.' What did 'possibly' mean? He would have lived if he hadn't gone. Although if she pointed that out Leon Aldridge would probably tell her that her father might have been knocked down by a bus.

'Gerald left the door open?' he said, making it a query. She had asked for Gerald and that had given him away, and someone had left the door open, and Gerald would admit it when the questioning started.

'He—came through into my uncle's flat,' she said slowly. 'He'd noticed my car and he came to say hello.'

'... Nice having you here,' Gerald had said, but this could change his mind ... She went on jerkily,

'And then he went out by our shop door, but of course he thought I'd bolt the connecting door, I said I would, and I *meant* to. He had no idea that I was——' She found herself wondering wildly how his nose had got broken. She wondered if anyone had hit him because he had stood listening to something they were stammering

42

out without any sign that he was hearing a word. Except that those ice blue eyes never flickered, and the stare was so intense it shrivelled you. 'So darn' nosey,' she finished lamely. 'And clumsy. I bumped against the thing it was standing on and the vase went over and—how much is it worth?' She held her breath.

'It isn't genuine,' he said. 'It's a background ornament.'

It would turn the hundreds into single figures. That meant she wouldn't have to sell the car and mortgage her future. 'Wow!' she said inadequately, 'that's a relief.'

'It is,' he said grimly, and Fran hastily resumed a downcast expression.

'How much, please?' she said.

'You'd better see Gerald about that.'

'Yes. All right. Again, I'm sorry—good morning.'

'Good morning.'

She wasn't risking knocking over anything else. She walked slowly and carefully back to the door. Once outside she ran like a rabbit. He wouldn't be watching her. He had turned away as he said good morning, but as she turned the corner she realised that if he had looked he would have seen her through one of the Gallery windows, and she had cut an undignified figure.

She had cut an undignified figure all along. Her face was flaming so that it must be matching her hair, although she hadn't done anything so very terrible.

She had been nosey and clumsy, but they weren't crimes, they were just being human. Of course Leon Aldridge didn't tolerate human failings. He was the ruthless one, and goodness, didn't he look it? The next time she came up against him she'd make sure she had nothing to apologise for.

She wondered they needed air-conditioning in the Gallery, when he could just walk around, spread a few sub-zero waves and cool the atmosphere.

She got back to the kitchen two minutes ahead of Uncle Ted, who thought her flushed face was pretty, and healthy, and that she made an altogether charming picture.

She didn't feel up to confessing about her nocturnal adventure. In an hour or two it might start to be ridiculous, so long as Gerald didn't get into trouble over it. But right now she couldn't have raised a smile.

The morning paper had arrived, together with three letters—two that looked like bills and one that had a typewritten envelope and a business letterhead. Uncle Ted opened them, placed the accounts on one side, and read the letter.

When Fran put a plate of bacon and eggs before him he came out of his preoccupation with a start. 'Forgive me, my dear, I'm so used to my own company that I've forgotten it's bad manners to read one's mail at the breakfast table.'

'Is it? I've never heard that.' In leisured times and leisured households maybe, but what a nonsense. 'You read them,' she said. 'Not that they look much fun. All business, are they?'

'I'm afraid so, and where's your breakfast?'

'I'm having toast.'

'But you always have a cooked breakfast at home.'

'That's because my mother insists.' She collected the toast that had popped up from the toaster and brought it to the table. 'Why do you think I left home?' she joked. 'So that I can please myself how much I eat for breakfast.'

'I got in the bacon especially for you,' he said reproachfully.

44

'And I'll join you sometimes, but you'll be getting the cooked breakfasts from now on. I shall enjoy bullying you to eat, there must be a lot of my mother in me.'

'No,' he said flatly, and Fran spread her toast and asked,

'Am I more like my father?'

'The hair, of course.' She hadn't put on any make-up this morning, and her face had a scrubbed endearing quality. The copper hair looked very bright, and her dark-lashed eyes were very green. 'You're one on your own,' he said.

'Which some might say was not a bad thing.' Gerald might be thinking that at this very minute. Fran could imagine how scathing Leon Aldridge would be to a member of his staff who left the Galleries open. Especially when the girl-next-door had taken advantage and blundered around by moonlight.

While they ate breakfast, and discussed the news headlines, her thoughts were on the Gallery and what was happening there.

Her uncle went down to open the crafts shop and she put on her make-up. Her hand was steadier now that she knew the vase wasn't valuable. She doubted if she could have applied lipstick and mascara before, but she managed it now. She was wearing jeans and sandals, and an emerald green T-shirt. She hoped she looked workmanlike, ready to get down to the job, because the flat, like the shop, needed a spring face-lift.

Uncle Ted had been shifting for himself since before Christmas, when his long-time cleaner-lady went off to help her sister run a boarding house in Brighton. The place was all right, but it lacked sparkle, and Fran was eager to start on it.

She got down as Uncle Ted was dragging the wooden

garden table out and took hold of one end, helping him set it in place in the small section of the forecourt that fronted the crafts shop. She hoped Gerald wouldn't come out of the Galleries while she was here with Uncle Ted, but she must see him as soon as she could, to apologise and try to explain.

While the T.R.7 that was Leon Aldridge's car was still parked she wasn't going into the Galleries. When that disappeared she must go in, and say she was sorry for causing trouble. In the meantime there was plenty to occupy her. The shop dealt in traditional regional crafts, from corn dollies to silverware. The customers were usually tourists, the season was just starting, and it wouldn't be Fran's fault if it wasn't a record.

Uncle Ted did look tired. The morning light showed that and she resolved to take care of him and lift as much strain from him as possible. She started on un-obtrusive tidying—she would do the cleaning and polishing when the shop was closed—and a little rearrangement of some of the wares.

Uncle Ted was all for it. He wanted her involved here, busy and happy. And perhaps she had inherited some of her father's artistic talent, she couldn't paint or draw, but she had a good eye for design. She also had youth and enthusiasm and Edward Reynolds watched her with wonder and amusement. A quicksilver girl with hair of flame.

'How about putting some of these outside?' she suggested, indicating the wood carving section. There was a bowl of 'worry' eggs, wooden animals, love spoons. Nothing expensive, and on the garden table they might catch the customers' eye and lure them into the fore-court and the shop.

'Yes, we could try that,' said Uncle Ted, and Fran was

46

completing her wooden display when Leon drove out from the arch leading to the car park. He stopped for pavement walkers, and looked across at Fran through his open window. She called,

'It's all right, I'm only putting them on this table. I'm not starting a street market.'

'I'm glad to hear it.' He didn't sound as though he thought that was funny, and she watched his car go, with its fleeting image of the man at the wheel, the fair straight hair, the greyness of his suit. Much more of you, she thought, and I'll be using a worry egg myself.

And now for Gerald and her apologies for last night. She went into the Galleries, and a youngish man she didn't know looked up hopefully. When she asked for Mr Maddox he took her to the door marked Manager, and tapped it for her.

'Come in,' Gerald called. He was behind a desk. As Fran walked in he got to his feet.

'Hello,' she said, hearing the door close behind her. 'I'm sorry.'

'Sit down.' Gerald was smiling wryly, he had obviously had his interview with Leon Aldridge, and Fran perched on the edge of a Chippendale chair. 'He came in early this morning,' said Gerald. 'He's gone to the airport now.'

'I'd no right to go gawping around. I feel dreadful.' She twisted her hands together. 'Was he very mad?'

'Put it like this,' said Gerald. 'He wasn't pleased. If I use that door again I come back and lock it from this side.'

'As far as I'm concerned,' she promised fervently, 'it's walled up. Nothing would get me through it again. I shall have nightmares about backing into the vase.' She wouldn't even have to be sleeping. She didn't think she

47

would ever see priceless Chinese porcelain with any real pleasure again. 'I thought about two thousand pounds,' she shuddered, and asked, 'How much was it worth?'

'The boss said not to bother.'

She didn't want to be beholden. She protested, 'I'd much rather pay for it.'

'You'd better see him when he gets back.'

It was no use arguing, if those were Leon Aldridge's instructions. 'All right,' she said, and stood up, and Gerald inquired,

'What are you doing this evening?'

'Staying home.'

'How about coming out with me?'

Fran looked at him with shining eyes. 'You *are* nice.' Her grin was quick and infectious. 'I thought last night would be the end of our beautiful friendship.'

'I hope not,' he said warmly. 'About tonight?'

'I don't think I should be leaving Uncle Ted the minute I get here, so to speak.'

'Can I look in tomorrow?'

'Of course.'

On Sunday afternoon they hired a boat, and chugged down river, past weeping willows and cows eyeing them from lush green meadows. The past months' rainfall had been high and the river ran deep, but there was sunshine on Sunday and Fran remembered her father rowing her over this stretch of river on summer days. He had loved the river, he had swum in it, but it had not prepared him for the currents around Sicily.

They passed the island on which the Aldridge house stood, reaching the bank by a bridge on one side, while on the other the river flowed. Gerald let the engine idle, looking at the house as though his connection with the firm gave him a proprietorial interest. 'Quite a place, isn't it?' he said proudly.

You couldn't see it too well for the trees, but what you could see was impressive. Fran said lightly, 'I'd have thought he'd have a drawbridge. Then he could raise it and no one could get near him.'

'He doesn't need a drawbridge,' said Gerald. She agreed, Leon Aldridge's eyes put up their own steel plate, but Gerald admired him, and when she asked,

'What's he like to work for?' Gerald said,

'Fantastic.'

She didn't want to be told that. She saw the wake of a water creature, and pointed it out and waited for it to surface. It was a vole, and the river really was an enchanting place.

Fran's first week went well. Uncle Ted was looking healthier. He was eating the meals she was cooking for him, and both the shop and the flat were brighter and in better order.

She enjoyed meeting customers, showing off the pretty things and the interesting things, telling them why this was lucky and how that was made. She was a natural salesgirl because she enjoyed selling; and Uncle Ted introduced her to a couple who delivered that week, one a schoolteacher who made lovely little handstitched samplers, the other a potter who brought a stack of mugs that Uncle Ted had ordered. They were nice people; she was sure that all the folk who dealt with the crafts shop were nice.

Every day was different, which was more than you could have said for being Arthur Deane's secretary, and every day was fun.

She saw quite a lot of Gerald. Working next door he

managed to pop round for coffee most days, and Wednesday and Saturday evenings she went out with him.

Saturday they went to the cinema and then came back to Fran's home with fish and chips for supper. She had her own key. She opened the side door and they went up the stairs to the flat. Voices reached them on the landing. Her uncle's first, and then another man's, at conversational pitch. She couldn't hear what was being said, but she recognised the voice and turned to Gerald and whispered, 'Is that Leon Aldridge?'

'Sounds like him.'

'What's he doing here?'

Gerald shrugged. 'He's often round here.'

'*Here?*' She was still whispering, so was Gerald. 'You mean in this flat?'

'Yes.'

Uncle Ted had said nothing about Leon Aldridge being on calling terms. 'Why?' she mouthed.

'I don't know,' Gerald mouthed back. 'Ask him,' and as she registered reluctance, 'or ask your uncle.'

# CHAPTER THREE

THE very first chance Fran had she would certainly ask her uncle why he hadn't told her that Leon Aldridge was 'always round here'. If she'd known that before she came she might have thought twice about coming. She would have come, but she hated opening the door and seeing him sitting there.

He looked so cool, so in charge as he stood up. As though she was walking into his house instead of the other way round, and the worried wrinkles were deep round Uncle Ted's eyes. Of course she wasn't going to insult a visitor, although she couldn't pretend she was glad to see him.

She said, 'Hello. We heard voices, but this is a surprise.'

'Good evening,' said Aldridge. He looked at Gerald briefly, then back at Fran, clutching her warm bundle of fish and chips and filling the room with their plebeian odour.

'Have you come about the vase?' she asked.

She had told Uncle Ted that tale and he had agreed she was lucky. She didn't really think it had brought Leon Aldridge round here on a Saturday night, and he said, 'No.'

'Just – dropped in? How nice.' She couldn't smile at him, she *couldn't*. She said, 'We weren't planning for you. You're welcome to a small cut off the fish and a few chips, but I shouldn't think fish and chips out of the paper are your dish.'

'I was just leaving,' he said, as though she had opened the door for him, and metaphorically speaking she had.

She wanted him to go. 'I'll see you out,' she said. She wanted to close the side door after him. If he had come through the Galleries she wanted to bolt that door.

He could have said he knew the way. Instead he said goodnight to the men and went ahead of her along the corridor and down the stairs. Fran caught up with him at the side door and said, 'About that vase.'

He opened the door and his face was cold and still in the moonlight. 'Give whatever you think to a charity,' he said.

'Charity?' she echoed. 'I shouldn't have thought you'd have gone much for charity.'

'How would you know what I go for?' he asked. 'Or what I eat.'

The door was shut again and she sat down for a moment on the wooden bench in the garden furniture set, because her legs were wobbling. Finding Leon Aldridge in Uncle Ted's flat had seemed a threat, as though his presence was a danger to that secure and happy place. She knew it was unfair to blame him because her father had broken up the first home she had ever known, but her instincts had been to get him out of here and bar the door on him.

Neither Uncle Ted nor Gerald was going to understand. It made no sense to herself, and she went back upstairs to find the two men exactly where she had left them. Uncle Ted was still sitting in his chair, Gerald was still standing by the table, and the fish and chips were still in their paper.

She smiled. 'Seems he doesn't like fish and chips,' she said. 'Do sit down, Gerald, I'll dish up.'

It wasn't a chatty supper. Gerald did his best, balancing a tray on his knee, discussing the film they had seen tonight, addressing remarks to Uncle Ted, who didn't answer as often as not. Uncle Ted was always polite, it was just that he wasn't listening, he was thinking.

When Gerald put down his tray, leaving half his supper, Fran wasn't surprised. There was a tense atmosphere here, and she couldn't blame a visitor for leaving.

'I'd better be on my way,' said Gerald, and Uncle Ted heard that.

'Goodnight then, my boy,' he said.

Fran went downstairs with Gerald. She said, 'I don't like your employer.'

'I know,' said Gerald. It had been quite a little scandal in its day. Some people might still remember it. He reached for her rather clumsily, patting her shoulder. 'Losing your father was a rotten thing to happen,' he said, 'but don't blame Leon. You're too nice a girl to be that unfair.'

'I don't blame him for anything,' she said. 'I just don't like him.'

Gerald thought she was being unreasonable, and upstairs Uncle Ted had stopped trying to eat his supper. His plate was by his feet, and he was sitting back in his armchair, looking wearier than he had all week.

Fran sat on the pouffe in front of the fire. She knew there was some talking to be done, so she started it by asking, 'Does he come round here often?'

'Yes.'

'Are you'—she hesitated—'friends?' and Uncle Ted paused for a moment before he said,

'Yes.'

Fran could imagine her mother's reaction to that. No wonder he had kept it quiet. He wouldn't have been welcome at the farm if Fran's mother had known he was matey with Leon Aldridge, although as the two men had worked next door to each other for more than ten years that was natural enough.

'There's no reason why not, of course,' said Fran. 'I'm sorry I wasn't more welcoming, but it was a shock—I didn't expect to see him here.'

'Friends and business colleagues,' Uncle Ted elaborated.

'Yes, of course. With the Galleries next door——'

'Closer than that, my dear,' he cut in, and she was puzzled until he explained, 'I only have a lease on this place and it doesn't have much longer to run.'

So Leon Aldridge owned the whole building. This had always been Uncle Ted's shop, he had bought it. She had never heard it mentioned that it wasn't freehold. She whispered, appalled, 'You mean he could take over?'

'No,' said Uncle Ted very quickly, 'he wouldn't do that,' and Fran felt that he was reassuring himself as much as her. 'But business hasn't been too healthy lately and I'm not getting any younger. Only a couple of weeks ago the doctor was telling me I ought to be taking a rest.'

She could believe that. She must see that doctor and hear what he had to say.

'Looking to the future,' said Uncle Ted, 'it would ease my mind if you and Leon got on together. He could keep this shop going.'

At what cost? What changes would he make? What kind of a going concern would it be once Leon Aldridge had a say in its future?

Fran said bitterly, 'You *do* mean he could take it over,' and was sorry as soon as the words were spoken, because Uncle Ted looked as hurt as though she had struck him. She wished she could have taken that back and she bit her lip, prepared to agree that she had spoken hastily if he told her again, 'He wouldn't do that.'

Instead he said, 'I thought if you came down here, you're an adult now, not a child—you're not your mother, your mother will always be a child in many ways—you'd realise how prejudiced you've been.'

'I know I'm prejudiced.' And she was sorry, prejudice was inexcusable although she tried to excuse herself. 'But I can't help it. I don't like him, any more than he likes me.'

'He doesn't dislike you.'

Why should he? She had never done him any harm, except for the vase, of course, and that wasn't worth much. 'Maybe he doesn't dislike me,' she said caustically. 'He's spoken to me, but I don't think he's ever seen me.'

'But he has.' Uncle Ted smiled then, and she smiled too, because she was glad to see him smiling again. 'He said he could understand Gerald forgetting to lock the connecting door. You were a girl who could make a man forget his own name.'

She didn't credit that for a minute. Uncle Ted was conning her; although Leon Aldridge might have said something vaguely complimentary because Fran was Uncle Ted's ewe lamb. But if he was prepared to be polite so was she. You didn't have to like a man to be civil to him.

She said gaily, 'I'll behave, honestly, next time we meet.'

'Tomorrow night,' said Uncle Ted. 'He's coming round to have a meal with us.'

Her spirits hit rock bottom. She felt her mouth and her shoulders droop. It was like being told, 'The dentist tomorrow, and two back stoppings.' 'Do I have to be here?' she pleaded, but that was why Uncle Ted had invited Leon Aldridge, so that he and Fran could meet socially.

Uncle Ted had business worries. Leon Aldridge was his landlord and perhaps his backer, and if Fran was going to be any use in the crafts shop, much less run it on her own, she must get on better terms with the owner of the Aldridge Galleries. She would have to be here because it meant so much to Uncle Ted, and on her best behaviour.

'What can we talk about?' she asked desperately. She didn't know enough about the business yet to keep up an informed conversation, and what else would interest the Iceman?

Her uncle smiled. 'You don't usually find it hard to talk.'

Fran talked to anyone, and she could get almost anyone talking to her. 'Usually no,' she agreed. 'To him, yes.'

'Because you are prejudiced.' They were back again at the root of the trouble. 'What about taking him as you find him?' Uncle Ted suggested. 'Starting tomorrow.'

If she could only brainwash herself that she was meeting a stranger she would have an open mind. Tonight she had made two impertinent assumptions—that Leon Aldridge was a snob and that he lacked charity, and, as he had pointed out, how would she know?

She began to gather up trays and plates—no one had eaten much—wondering, 'What shall we have tomorrow night? I can't do any more shopping, it's Sunday. What does he eat?'

'Food,' said Uncle Ted, with a twinkle. 'He is human, you know.'

'Oh, you,' she said. 'A lot of help you are!'

A business colleague of Uncle Ted's was coming to supper, and she would put on as good as meal as she could at such short notice. Then she would sit quietly by and let them do the talking, keep her ears open and maybe learn what the situation really was.

She had phoned home this morning and told her mother she was enjoying the work, and she was dating the young man she had gone around with the last time she was here. Her mother had remembered Gerald, and had asked, 'He isn't married?' Reassured on that she had said, 'That's nice.' But Fran wondered now what her mother would say if she had been told, 'I'm cooking a meal for Leon Aldridge tomorrow, and I hope it's only a business truce that Uncle Ted has in mind. It would be gruesome if he was matchmaking.'

She was sure that such an idea had never crossed Uncle Ted's mind. That was entirely her mother's province, and Leon Aldridge was the last man her mother would consider. Uncle Ted simply wanted an end to Fran's old antagonism, and so did Fran. It didn't matter when she never saw Leon Aldridge, but it would be awkward when he might pop up any minute. Bad for business, according to Uncle Ted; and not much good for Fran's nervous system.

The meal would have been their Sunday dinner, which they would have eaten midday. She cooked the menu she had planned for seven-thirty in the evening instead. Nothing fancy, an ordinary traditional rib of beef with Yorkshire pudding, roast potatoes and spring greens, with gooseberry tart and cream to follow.

Uncle Ted had produced a bottle of wine that was warming to room temperature, and Fran was in the last stages of preparation in the kitchen. She was wearing a long skirt in bright patchwork cotton, and a white cotton blouse, with drawstrings at throat and wrists; and a bibbed white apron covering all.

Uncle Ted was laying the table in the living room, and

with kitchen and living room doors open Fran chatted away, raising her voice so that he could hear her.

Every time she started to feel apprehensive she told herself firmly, 'A stranger is coming. I've seen him before, but I know next to nothing about him, and he's a friend of Uncle Ted's so he can't be too bad.'

Her uncle passed the kitchen door and went down the stairs into the shop, and Fran stopped what she was doing—carving the meat—to listen in case he'd heard the door bell and she hadn't. But there were no voices and she went on carving.

At twenty-five past seven she had the meal ready for serving and as she took off her apron a bell did ring, the phone bell in the office behind the shop.

She expected the ringing to stop as her uncle answered the phone, but it went on, and she figured that he must have come back up here and gone up the next flight of stairs to his bedroom. If he heard the phone he was leaving it to her, so she called, 'Uncle Ted, phone!' and plunged down the stairs, switching on a light and hurrying into the office.

'Hello,' she gasped into the receiver.

'Uncle Ted here,' said the receiver, and she goggled at it. 'I've just popped out to see a friend,' he went on blithely, 'and I've got caught up. I'll be along later.'

'*What?*'

'Start the meal without me,' and she was left babbling at the dialling signal.

'Where are you? What do you mean, you've got caught up?' When she put down the phone she still went on, as though he could hear her, 'You can't do this. You can't leave me to deal with him on my own!'

What was he playing at, pitching her into a tête-à-tête with Leon Aldridge? What did he imagine that would achieve? Well, if he was out she was out. She wouldn't answer the door. Uncle Ted had invited the man, she hadn't.

Right on time the doorbell rang and she knew she had to answer it. She was down here with lights on all over the place, but when Uncle Ted did put in an appearance she'd have plenty to say to him. It would serve him right if she took the early light back to Yorkshire in the morning.

Leon Aldridge was wearing a thin black polo-necked sweater and a grey suit. He didn't smile, of course. He looked at Fran with that impassive scrutiny that might have disconcerted her if she hadn't been fuming over Uncle Ted. She said, 'I don't know where my uncle's gone, but he isn't here. He vanished while I was in the kitchen, and he's just this minute phoned to say he'll be along later.'

'Would you rather I came back later?'

She was blocking his way, but to have agreed to that suggestion would have been like saying she was afraid to be alone with him, which would be ludicrous and insulting. She moved reluctantly, opening the door wider so that he could step past her. 'Of course not,' she said stiffly.

She told herself again, 'He's a businessman whom Uncle Ted knows well, but whom I'm meeting for the first time,' and led the way upstairs. 'Is it raining again?' she asked. She had heard it on the windows and seen it as a background when he stood in the doorway.

He said it was and they went into the living room, where the table was laid for three, and the moment he had finished laying it Uncle Ted had taken himself off.

'Will you have a drink?' Fran offered mechanically. 'A sherry? Do sit down.'

'Thank you.'

She poured two glasses, very pale and dry—much too dry for her taste but exactly his, she'd bet—and handed him one. They sat facing each other in the matching wicker armchairs, which were comfortable but hardly smart. She smoothed her skirt and would have liked to smooth her hair, she knew it was unruly from all this dashing, and she realised that she was still wearing her apron.

She took a gulp of her sherry and went on with her role of hostess. 'I went by your home last Sunday,' she told him brightly. 'The island. The river's high, isn't it, with all this rain?'

'Exceptionally.' He didn't drink. He sat there looking at her, then he said abruptly, 'I asked your uncle if he'd let me speak to you alone.'

Fran blinked her thick dark lashes. So this was a plot between Leon Aldridge and Uncle Ted. 'Why?'

His eyes seemed darker and the line between them deeper. His voice, she thought, was huskier. 'I know that you hold me responsible for what your father did,' he said, 'and also, I suppose, for what happened to him.'

She should have said, 'Of course not,' but she said what first came into her mind : 'How do you know?'

'Your mother blamed me. Your uncle told me how you feel, and you haven't tried to hide it.'

Fran was struck dumb. This was completely unexpected. She had always known that her feelings were irrational, but she couldn't think what to say. She sat miserably silent and Leon went on, 'He brought his work to me several times. He had talent, but he was getting nowhere. He was into his thirties, he had a job that he hated, and I told him to go somewhere where he *could* paint.'

He was appealing for her understanding. 'The accident was a tragedy,' he said, and she couldn't doubt that he meant it.

She said slowly, the admission dragged out of her, 'It could have happened here.'

'Your mother didn't believe that.' Her mother had called him a murderer in the gallery that morning long ago. That had been a terrible scene. He was remembering it now, Fran felt, and she said,

'I know he couldn't paint at home. The advice you gave him was sound.'

Now that Leon Aldridge had expressed regret it was easier to see him as a human being, instead of an iceman. He still had an impassive face, but when he said, 'Thank you,' she could read relief, as though she had taken a weight off his mind, and she began to smile.

He smiled back, and the smile transformed him. Sweet and devilish, it radiated an astounding charm, so that Fran opened her eyes wide.

'I've never seen you smile before,' she said.

'I've never seen you smile either.'

As she was the one who went around grinning like a Cheshire cat it seemed impossible that there was someone who had never seen a smile on her face. She wondered how much her smile changed her. Not drastically, she thought. 'Oh dear,' she said. 'Well, let's start from here.' She put down her glass and walked across to him holding out her hand. 'How do you do, Mr Aldridge. My uncle tells me you're a friend of his. I'm very glad to meet you.'

He stood too, tall and elegant. 'This is a great pleasure. Do you think you could call me Leon, and may I call you Fran?'

'Please do. After all, we are neighbours.'

He had taken the hand she offered, and they shook gravely. She could feel the strength in his hand although it was the lightest of pressures, and she was aware of the taut athletic build of his body. She was looking at him for the first time without prejudice, and he was something to look at.

'Shall we eat?' she said. 'The meal's ready and Uncle Ted said we were to start.' She added grimly, 'It would serve him right if we ate the lot, and drank all his wine.'

But the plan had worked out well. She was released from that childhood bitterness, and getting to know Leon Aldridge promised to be exciting. This really was a first meeting, and she had the confidence of a girl whom most men found attractive.

'I'm grateful to him,' said Leon. 'I think we should leave his share.'

'His plate can stay in the oven,' she said gaily. 'But we're starting ours. I don't know about you, but I'm hungry. Would you see to the wine while I dish up?'

Uncle Ted didn't go in for vegetable dishes, although there were dishes galore down in the shop. Up here he had always served his own meals straight on to the plate, and so did Fran. She had deliberately cut out the frills on this meal for Leon, but now she began to wish that the fare had been less hearty and more unusual. Even that there had been candles on the table, instead of the choice between electric light or firelight, too much or too little.

She carried in the plates and apologised, 'This isn't a very ambitious meal, but I didn't have much warning.'

'It looks delicious.' It was all right. As Dr Johnson once said, 'A good dinner enough ... but not a dinner to *ask* a man to.'

But Leon seemed to be enjoying it. He asked, 'Are you fond of cooking?'

'I don't know, I haven't done much. My mother's a good cook, I'm not a bad one.'

The Yorkshire pudding had come out just right, and that was a favourite with Uncle Ted. Fran hoped he would be home before it became indigestible. On the other hand, this twosome could develop more interest than a threesome.

'I've been feeding Uncle Ted up since I came,' she said, 'I was shocked when I saw him. He didn't look well at all to me. He's been worrying, I think. He says business isn't too good.'

She looked inquiringly at Leon, who took a sip of wine. So she asked him outright, 'Is it the general recession or is it the crafts shop in particular?'

'These are hard times,' he said, which everybody knew, 'but Ted does have his problems,' and before she could ask, 'What problems?' he was asking her, 'You haven't worked in a shop before, have you?'

He wasn't going to discuss Uncle Ted's circumstances and she had to let it go, following the new twist in the conversation. 'I've always been a secretary. Nothing very thrilling. I ended up at an estate agents.'

That sounded aimless, and she hadn't got as much satisfaction from any of her other jobs as she was finding in the crafts shop. 'I suppose you always knew what you were going to do.' She sounded a little wistful.

'The Galleries were always waiting,' he said.

She could imagine the satisfaction that gave him, knowing how he had enlarged their scope and made their name a power in the art world. She supposed that for her the crafts shop had always been waiting, but it was hardly the same thing. She wasn't going to build an empire on that, especially if the lease ran out.

He was watching her and she knew how easy it was to

read her face. She didn't want him asking what was making her scowl. The lease was Uncle Ted's business so long as all went well. If there were troubles then Fran would pitch in for all she was worth, but of course there would be no trouble, and she smiled broadly.

'That big statue, on the ground floor.' She gestured vaguely, sketching it in the air. 'I saw it from the balcony and it looked very odd. What's it supposed to be, exactly?'

It wasn't a statue so much as a huge rock, carved into a strange fluid shape. 'It's called Windrode,' he said.

'Does that mean anything?'

'It's a nautical term. It means riding the wind at anchor.'

'Oh!' Fran tried out the name against her memory of the work. Her expression made him smile. 'Well,' she said dubiously, 'I only saw it by moonlight, but I couldn't imagine it in my drawing room.'

She didn't have a drawing room, and the thing was as high as a bungalow. 'Neither did the artist,' said Leon. 'In a garden, now——'

'Ah yes, a garden.' She leaned across the table towards him, her green eyes sparkling. 'When you sell it send the customer round to us afterwards. Tell them we've got some gorgeous garden benches in natural elm. They can buy a bench to sit on and look at their statue.'

'And if you sell a bench send them to me for the statue.'

'It's a deal. How much is the statue?'

'A thousand.'

'Reasonable. You could almost say dirt cheap.' She pulled a grimace of exaggerated approval. 'Oh, I'm sure I can get rid of that for you.'

They laughed at each other, and he said, 'Your hair is an incredible colour.'

'Red.'

'Flame.' The electric light overhead shone down on her so that her hair was aureoled, and when she moved her head the copper glinted gold.

His hair was so fair it was almost silver, fine and straight, flopping over his forehead. The mouth was strong and clean cut. The toughness was there, like steel, but without that slight thickening of the bridge of the nose he could have modelled for a statue from Ancient Greece.

'How did your——' Fran began, then checked herself. He waited for her to go on, then said,

'How did what?'

She had been going to ask, 'How did your nose get broken?' but suppose it wasn't broken and this was its natural shape, then that would be a tactless question. Although if he was sensitive about it he would surely have had it straightened.

'How did I break my nose?' he said.

'Well, yes.'

'I fell out of a tree, when I was much younger.'

She could imagine him as a boy if she tried, but it was harder to imagine him clambering up trees. She grinned, 'I should hope you were younger, it's no way for a distinguished art dealer to go on. What were you doing in a tree?'

'Trying to get to the top,' he said solemnly.

'But you didn't?'

'Not that day.'

One day, while he was still a boy. He wouldn't give up. She said, 'I'd have forgotten about reaching the top if that had happened to me.'

'But, looking at your nose, it's obvious you've never fallen out of a tree.'

She had a pretty nose, neat and small and straight, and she found herself blushing slightly, as though no one had ever paid her a compliment before.

'When I did I landed on my feet,' she quipped. 'I've cat's eyes, haven't you noticed?'

He had been looking into her eyes. She had known long ago that his eyes were blue, but tonight she would not have described them as Arctic. 'And they see in the dark,' he said. 'Sometimes.'

He was talking about her tour of the Galleries on her first night here. She had wondered if she would ever manage to see the funny side of that and now, suddenly, it was a joke and she laughed. 'I was just looking at the pictures, that was why I bumped into the vase.'

'The painting that reminded you of your father's work?' She nodded. 'Would you like to see it properly?'

'Very much.'

'Shall we go round?'

They had eaten as they talked, the first course had almost disappeared. Fran would have let the gooseberry tart wait and gone round to the Galleries now, she always had had this tendency to rush things. Leon, she felt, would expect to finish his meal first, and then go calmly, without fuss. He was not an impulsive man, not one whose arm you could grab and say, 'Come on!'

But she brought in the dessert promptly and suggested, 'We could have coffee later.' When her plate was empty she wrote a note on the back of an envelope. 'Gone next door, Fran,' in case Uncle Ted returned before they did, and in case he had gone out without his key. She found a drawing pin in the office, and pinned the envelope to the side door.

The rain was a fine drizzle as they hurried from door to door, and once inside the Galleries Leon switched on lights, placed to illuminate the exhibits, so that Fran stood looking around her for a moment, eyes darting.

The central sculpture dominated the ground floor, and she stared up at it, asking, 'You were joking about the price?'

'No.'

'*No?* Do you mind if I laugh?'

'Not at all.'

When you looked hard at it it was certainly impressive, and she said slowly, 'In the right setting, I suppose, it would be rather exciting.'

'The picture you saw is upstairs?'

'Yes.'

They went up the staircase and along the balcony, to stand in front of the painting that had lured her through that connecting door. The similarity was even less by clearer light. Looking at it now she wondered how she could have mistaken it for her father's, and she said, 'Not so close, is it?'

'I can see what you meant,' he said.

She wished it had been. She wished she could have bought something to show for that lost year. She clasped her hands in a tight little grip, and her voice was tight, too controlled.

'We only have one of his paintings,' she said, looking at the painting on the wall but seeing the picture that hung in the living room at the farm.

'It was in my bedroom, my mother didn't like them around in those days. When he went I hid it, I think she might have destroyed it. She didn't ask about it. I brought it out after he died and now it has pride of place at the farm.'

She smiled, hiding sadness, 'She's proud of it now, she shows it to everybody. She's forgotten it was mine, that he gave it to me. He always gave his pictures away, and of course they were never worth much, were they—not in money, I mean? No one really valued him.'

'They would have done,' Leon said, and she blinked on a mist of tears.

'If he hadn't gone swimming that day. If the currents had been different. If he hadn't had cramp or whatever it was that happened. If . . .' She moved away and he said,

'I'm sorry,' and that made her turn back.

'I'm not blaming you.' She shouldn't have given way to that moment of bleakness. She put her hand on his arm in a spontaneous gesture of reassurance, not sure whether he was tense or if the muscles in his arm were iron-hard.

He said, 'If I can get hold of any of his pictures for you I will.'

'Thank you.'

He took her along the row of paintings, telling her a little about each artist, each painting. He showed her the sculpture—like the paintings there was traditional and modern—and in one of the rooms was some work ready for an exhibition in two weeks' time.

These pictures had an almost Japanese delicacy that made everyday objects strange and beautiful. 'They're exquisite,' she said.

'I think so.'

'Who painted them?'

'A woman who found she could paint when the children grew up.'

'They must be proud of her,' said Fran. 'Thank you for showing me around.'

'It's been a pleasure,' and he said that as though he

meant it.

The note had gone from the side door, and upstairs Uncle Ted was finishing his dinner. 'I've been looking round the gallery by invitation this time,' Fran told him, and his smile was smug, although he didn't actually say, 'I told you so.'

'And where have you been?' she asked.

'Up the road to see an old friend,' he said nonchalantly.

'That was very sneaky.' She smiled at both of them. 'Coffee?'

She made it and they sat together around the fire, the men in the wicker armchairs, Fran on the pouffe. She was glad her mother couldn't see them, but so far as Fran herself went it was a very comfortable arrangement.

There was no business talk. She had thought there might be, but there wasn't, and she didn't see how she could drag the future of the crafts shop into the conversation, unless she got some sort of opening. The Sunday papers were there and they talked around the headlines, with Uncle Ted doing most of the talking and in fine form.

He was in such good humour that he went off into rambling anecdotes like the absent-minded professor he might well have been. He had a scholar's wit, and he sat back in his chair, tapping the tips of his fingers together, funny and happy, and Fran felt again that protectiveness that had brought her dashing down here. She wanted to keep him happy, he was such a dear good man.

When Leon got up to go she was sorry the evening had to end, but it was work tomorrow. She went downstairs a couple of steps ahead of him and at the door he said, 'Goodnight, and thank you.' Not just for the meal, he meant, but for admitting that he was not to blame for the past.

She smiled. 'See you,' she said.

'Yes.' He didn't touch her in passing her, but when she closed the door behind him she realised that her heart was pounding as though she expected him to kiss her. Most men might have done, tonight had got off to a promising start for the future. He found her attractive, she was sure of that, but he hadn't kissed her goodnight. She hadn't expected him to, she told herself. He was a very attractive man, but he was also a very cool customer.

Uncle Ted was whistling softly to himself, clearing away the coffee cups. 'You see,' he said, 'I knew you two would get on all right together.'

'Oh, you're smart. But don't start dashing around because the doctor did say you should be taking it easy!' She took the tray from him. 'At least, that's what you told me.'

'All right.' It was getting late, and he looked surprised as though he had suddenly realised he was tired. 'I think I will go up,' he said. He kissed her cheek. 'You won't be long, will you?'

'Five minutes. See you in the morning. Sleep well.'

He walked out of the room briskly, but his step was slow on the stairs and she thought again—I must talk to that doctor ...

Fran was serving in the shop next morning when the roses came. She was wrapping up a loving spoon, and telling her two customers the way to the nearest café where they could get home-made cakes, when the man came in carrying a cellophane-covered bouquet and asked, 'Miss Reynolds?'

'Yes.'

70

'For you.' He handed them over as though they were his own idea, and went off whistling.

'Roses!' breathed the woman who had bought the loving spoon. 'I just love roses.'

They were peach-coloured buds, just opening, and Fran fumbled with the packaging in feverish haste to get at the little white card. It said, 'Thank you again, Leon.'

She was pleased about that. They might have been from Arthur. He had written to her last week and she hadn't answered his letter yet. Uncle Ted would be tickled pink, he was in the office, and she picked them up to take along and show him.

As she passed the door leading outside Gerald came in, almost bumping into her with her arms full of roses.

'Is it your birthday?' he asked. 'I saw the van.'

'Er—no.'

She had the little white card between her thumb and finger. He leaned closer and read it and said, 'Thank you for what?'

'He came round here for a meal last night.'

'It must have been some meal.'

'Fair to middling.' She didn't want trouble with Gerald, she never wanted trouble, but from the way his glasses were gleaming he wasn't thrilled about her roses.

'I thought you didn't like him,' he said.

'I think I've changed my mind.'

'Have you?' He breathed deeply. 'Then I think you ought to know that he's an expert all round, and he collects more than pictures.'

'Does he?' she said. He was waiting for her to say something, and nothing brighter came to mind.

Gerald looked at the roses and then at her, speaking quietly, almost as though he was sorry for her. 'Just watch out he doesn't add you to his collection.'

# CHAPTER FOUR

FRAN hadn't imagined she was the first girl to whom Leon had sent roses. He must be—thirty-four? and eligible in every way, and hardly an iceman after all. 'Thanks for the warning,' she said. 'I'll watch out.'

In the office Uncle Ted was typing a letter on an ancient machine. Fran was a better typist and could probably have handled the clerical work more efficiently, but so far he had preferred her to concentrate on dealing with the public. She was a breath of fresh air in the shop, he said.

Now she held out her bouquet of roses and said, 'Look what I've got. Aren't they beautiful?'

'Very fragrant.' He sniffed one obligingly, and asked, 'Who sent you these?'

She showed him the card and he beamed. She was glad he was pleased. Gerald had banged out of the shop as she came into the office, and that was a nuisance. He wasn't likely to complain to Leon, but it looked as though he was considering himself an injured party.

Fran had had trouble with jealous boy-friends before. Perhaps she didn't look the faithful kind but, like Arthur, the men she went around with often took too much for granted, and expected exclusive rights to her company.

Sometimes it was crazy. She had once actually found herself in the middle of a fist fight. She was eighteen and a studious young man had taken her to the cricket club dance, and resented her dancing with anyone else. Fran was happily unaware he was smouldering until he erupted, and swung a wild right at his rival, who promptly knocked him flat.

Her mother was very upset about that. Mrs Boyd, the mother of Fran's escort, was a friend of Isabel's, and Graham was a nice quiet boy who had never been in any trouble at all. 'Until he started to go out with Fran,' Mrs Boyd had said, as though that had pitched him straight into a life of crime.

Jim had burst out laughing when he was told, Uncle Ted had thought it was funny too, but it had been a long time before Isabel and Mrs Boyd spoke to each other again, and from then on Fran had become wary at any sign of possessiveness.

She couldn't imagine Leon being possessive. He was much too civilised, and a cool man around would be a welcome change.

He came into the shop that afternoon. There were several customers browsing around. Fran was with two American girls who were trying on clothes, and looking at themselves in the long mirror on the wall.

There was a miniature boutique of woven garments in a little alcove, and a Victorian screen for changing behind. They were trying on cloaks, and when Fran turned and smiled at Leon they turned to look. 'Thank you for the roses,' she said.

'I'm glad you liked them. I wondered if you'd care to come to the theatre tonight.'

Yes, she thought, I would. He was in a denim shirt again, and the beige trousers. His voice was quiet and cultured, he was in no way obtrusive, but she knew exactly what his impact was on the two girls standing beside her. They didn't know he ran an empire, but Fran heard them gasp. She looked across at Uncle Ted, who was showing a customer a range of pewter tankards, and Uncle Ted said, 'Yes, my dear, you go.'

'All right,' said Fran. 'I'd like that.'

'I'll see you at seven,' said Leon.

'I wouldn't have waited for Dad's O.K. if he'd asked me,' laughed one of the girls so that Leon heard her, but he didn't turn and smile, and they went back to looking at themselves in their cloaks while Fran took down a skirt.

It was ankle-length in fine black wool, with a scarlet pattern of geometric flowers, and the girl who was considering a scarlet cloak said, 'That matches.'

Fran grinned, 'I've just treated myself to it, for tonight, but we do have some smashing skirts.'

She sold them a cloak and a skirt each, and Uncle Ted said of course she could have the skirt with the scarlet flowers. By the time this shop shut the other shops in town would be closing too, and although she had brought an adequate little wardrobe with her she fancied something new for tonight.

Goodness knows this was an occasion, a date with Leon Aldridge. Again she baulked from imagining what her mother would have to say if she heard, but by blotting out her childhood memories Fran was finding Leon a man of compelling charm.

She was looking forward to tonight, and the thrill of challenge had something to do with it. Her admirers to date had been uncomplicated, she had provided the excitement in their lives. Leon was different. Fran wasn't going to bowl him over, but it might be amusing to try.

She had a black velvet waistcoat which complemented the skirt, showing bare arms, smooth throat, and the shadow between firm young breasts. She made up skilfully, put on very small single pearl earrings, and thought she looked well enough.

Uncle Ted said she was a picture. He was biased, of course, and delighted that she was dressed up and waiting for Leon. She sat with him, watching the early evening news, and feeling a fluttering of apprehension that was unusual for her.

When the doorbell rang she sat bolt upright, clutching the chair arms with fingers that seemed unwilling to let go, so that she could get up and walk downstairs and open the door to Leon. After a moment Uncle Ted said, 'The bell.'

She jumped up then. 'Yes, I heard it—'bye for now.'

'Enjoy yourselves,' he said benignly, as though he was saying, 'Bless you, my children.'

Fran picked up her coat and handbag from the settee and hurried, expecting the bell to start ringing again. Most people ring again after they have waited for a minute. But it didn't ring, and it was Leon who was waiting.

He looked dark. It was a dark night and he was wearing a dark suit. The silver-fair hair, and the light tan of his skin, contrasted sharply. 'Ready?' he said.

'Ready and waiting.' She was struggling into her coat, and he held it for her to get her arms in, but left her to do the buttoning up herself.

'I'm sorry if I kept you waiting,' he said.

He had rung the bell at exactly the time he was expected, and last night too. This time last night Fran had been cooking the dinner, and dreading the moment he would walk into the house. There was a radical change in only twenty-four hours.

She said, 'You didn't. Just a cliché.' She peered out into the cold air. 'Do we walk it?'

It was only about ten minutes' walk to the theatre, but it was dark and damp, and when he said, 'I don't think so,' she was glad to make for the car park behind the building. Uncle Ted's car had its usual spot, up against the wall, and Fran's Mini stood close to Leon's car.

They were an ill matched pair and she laughed, 'Bit like the Galleries and the crafts shop, aren't they? I hope your car doesn't give mine an inferiority complex.' She patted the bonnet of the car. 'Never you mind, Poppy.'

'Poppy?' Leon echoed.

'She's always been Poppy. It seems to suit her.'

'Was it ever red?'

'No. She came in this colour.' The colour was green and Leon said,

'I give up.'

'I bet you don't,' said Fran gaily. 'But Poppy's very easily hurt, so how about us taking her along tonight?'

She wouldn't have been surprised if he had preferred his own car. Poppy was rather a scruff, but he said what she was thinking, 'It would be easier to park,' and she fumbled for her car keys in her handbag.

Leon took the passenger seat beside her, long legs jack-knifed, saying nothing while she pulled out the choke and turned the ignition key to a series of discouraging clicks.

'I haven't used her for a week,' she explained defensively, 'and you know how damp it's been.' She pushed the choke half in, she didn't want to flood the carburettor, tried again and got another click.

'Is Poppy going to take it personally if we use my car?' Leon asked at last, and as he spoke the engine spluttered, coughed and caught, with Fran getting into gear fast before it could stall again.

'Very female,' said Leon.

'I suppose males never wait till the last minute before making a move.' She felt him laugh silently beside her as she drove out through the archway.

It was a short journey, but she was glad she was driving because that meant she had to keep her mind on the hazards of the road. Just sitting, with him driving, she might have been too conscious of him for comfort in this confined space. She thought—trying to smile at herself—I feel as though I have a panther riding with me. I feel as though there isn't enough air and I have to breathe faster.

She said, 'I don't suppose we'll be able to park in front of the theatre, it's usually full there, isn't it? We'll try farther along the road, shall we?'

They were lucky. There was a small space, near and handy, just big enough for a little car like Poppy, and Fran edged in. She opened her door and got out, and Leon came round to meet her.

He took her arm as they went into the foyer, where the crowd of tonight's theatregoers was milling around. They were nearly all tourists; this was one of the things they came to Stratford for, to see one of Shakespeare's plays. Most of them were in holiday mood, chattering, laughing.

Leon took her coat and went off with it towards Cloaks, and Fran watched the audience as though they were part of the play. She always did enjoy the time before the curtain went up.

Some of the men gave her second looks, her bright hair was an eye-catcher, and she was a pretty girl. But she got much less attention than Leon did. He was tall, strikingly distinguished, and he moved with arrogance and grace.

She watched the effect he had, crossing the foyer towards her, although he seemed to neither know nor care. That was true arrogance, not to care how you looked to anyone else. Fran was appreciative of being appreciated. She smiled back when anyone smiled at her, within reason, of course. But Leon's smiles were few, and he reached her without stopping, or speaking, or smiling at anyone. But as an escort she had no complaints against him at all. He was attentive, concentrating entirely on her until the curtain rose. She was almost sorry when they had to settle down and watch the play, because it might have been more fun to have gone on talking.

The play was one of the doleful ones, and as the agony thickened on stage she looked surreptitiously around for a little light relief. Leon, in profile beside her, was interesting to study, out of the corner of her eye. She could hardly turn in her seat and stare at him without him turning too to see what she was up to.

He'd make a good Hamlet, she thought, except that Hamlet was a dreamer, not a doer. Or a Romeo maybe, if Romeo had fallen off that balcony on to his nose.

She swallowed on a giggle, turning it into a cough—there were no giggles in this play. But the cover-up couldn't have been too convincing because in the interval, while they were sitting in the bar, Leon asked her, 'What were you laughing at just now?'

She said airily, 'I was thinking you look like an actor.'

'And?'

'And—the sort of roles your face might fit.'

'Such as?'

'Hamlet?'

'The gloomy Dane?'

She laughed at him. 'You don't smile that much, do you?'

That made him smile. 'No,' he said, agreeing with her, and she went cheerfully on,

'Romeo perhaps, if Romeo had fallen off the balcony.'

'Instead of out of a tree?' He shook his head. 'I don't see myself as Romeo.'

'Who died for love?' She made her voice theatrically tremulous, then shook her head too. 'On second thoughts, not Romeo.'

'Now you'd look the part for Rosalind.' That was a compliment, Rosalind was probably the most famed and fascinating of Shakespeare's women, but Fran raised astonished eyebrows.

'You mean I could pass for a boy?' knowing that the cut of her waistcoat revealed her as all girl, and Leon chuckled,

'Not even from the back of the stalls.' They were both laughing when a girl said,

'What's the joke, darling?'

Her softly waved, beautifully cut hair was as fair as Leon's. Her face was pale and perfect, and smooth as though she had never had a care in her life. She stood by Leon, her hand on his shoulder—as expensively dressed as he was, in a silk striped grey-and-blue tabard and skirt—and Fran's first impression was: they look like a picture in a glossy magazine, well bred beautiful people, advertising something very pricey.

That was immediately followed by a reaction of dislike, because the girl was looking daggers at her. Lips curled sardonically, there was nothing friendly in that smile.

'Hello,' said Fran, chin tilted.

'This is Judith Waring,' said Leon. 'Judith, Fran Reynolds.'

'The crafts shop girl,' said Judith, and Fran wondered how she knew, and come to that who she was.

'Yes,' she said.

Judith looked her up and down. 'Is that a homespun skirt?'

Fran smiled brilliantly, 'Of course.' She touched her tiny pearl earrings. 'And I dived for these as well.'

Judith went on smiling with closed lips. 'Aren't you clever?' She looked pointedly at Leon, who was sitting imperturbably sipping his drink. 'And you'll need to be,' she said.

She went back to a little group at the bar who were waiting for her and Fran said, 'Don't tell me what I've done to her, I can guess. I'm here with you.'

Leon shrugged, not in the least put out, and she wondered what it would take to embarrass him. More than a jealous girl-friend, and that was what Judith Waring was, of course.

'Who is she?' Fran was about to ask. 'What does she do for a living that gives her the right to sneer at the crafts shop as though it was stocked by ham-fisted amateurs?' But that was when the back-to-your-seats bell rang, so she said instead, 'Saved by the bell!' and Leon finished his drink and stood up.

Saved by nothing, she thought. You might have told me what Judith Waring does for a living, but you would not have discussed her, or explained or excused.

She looked for Judith again in the crowds leaving the theatre, although she didn't particularly want to see her. But sure enough there she was, in a three-quarter pale mink jacket, belted with casual elegance. Real mink, of course. Fran couldn't claim to be able to recognise real from phoney out of touching distance, but she knew that Judith wore nothing but the best.

A pale gloved hand waved at them and Leon nodded back while Fran grinned graciously from ear to ear, not to be outdone, and nearly slipped off the step. If Leon hadn't had a hand under her elbow she would have measured her length, and Judith would have loved that.

'Thanks,' Fran muttered.

They walked along the pavement towards the parked Poppy and she asked, 'Will you come back for a coffee?'

'Is your uncle expecting you back so soon? I've booked a table.'

'Oh, lovely! Yes, that's all right.' Perhaps she had better phone Uncle Ted and warn him, he might want to go to bed if she was going to be out till midnight or so. Or she could look in and tell him. Or phone from where they were eating. She asked, 'Where are we going?'

He told her. It was about ten miles away and she hadn't been there. There weren't many places around here that she had been, she had left too soon and returned too rarely. Now around the farm she had tried out every good eating house within a twenty-mile radius.

'Shall I drive?' Leon suggested as she opened the passenger door.

'Don't you like being driven?'

'No.'

'Male chauvinism?' She hadn't crashed any gears getting him here, and she had parked neatly, but she was prepared to hear he was against women drivers.

'It's not personal,' he said. 'You're an excellent driver.'

'But you don't really trust anyone else at the controls?' She wasn't only talking about cars, and when he said slowly,

'I suppose I don't,' neither was he.

'Well, I don't mind being a passenger.' She slid into the passenger seat and reached to open the driver's door. 'Up to a point,' she said as he got in beside her. She liked to be in charge of her life too. She was used to getting her own way.

She sat back and watched him. She didn't tell him about Poppy's little tricks, let him figure them out for himself. To begin with this wasn't the easiest car to get into reverse. You could be certain the reverse gear had locked and still sail forward, and if he did they'd be up on the pavement. There was no one walking here right now so it wouldn't matter and might take him down a peg.

But he reversed smoothly and competently, and off they went with no more than Poppy's usual bangs and rattles.

'What does Judith do?' Fran asked, surprised to find that uppermost in her mind as soon as there was a quiet moment.

'Do?' Leon echoed.

'I mean what's her job, her profession?' She sounded tart, and why not? Judith had sounded as though Fran's job was a joke.

'She's a designer, wallpapers, textiles.'

'And very successful from the looks of her. Does she live round here?'

'Most of the time.'

An art expert and a top designer should make a compatible pair, so Judith and Leon had more in common than dazzling good looks, and Fran was consumed with curiosity, although she had never probed into anyone else's affairs before. What she was wondering was, 'When did you last make love to her?' She couldn't ask that, but it stayed at the back of her mind.

She said, 'I hear you collect more than pictures. I was told to watch out I didn't get pinned down in your collection.'

'Who warned you?' He sounded amused. 'Gerald?'

'Why pick on him?'

'Because you've got him pinned down already.'

'I hope not.' She spoke more emphatically than she knew. 'I'm no collector,' she said.

'No?' He gave her a quick sidewards grin. 'According to your uncle you left a job lot of them in Yorkshire, pinned down with needles through their hearts.'

'The scandalous old gossip!' She wouldn't have believed it of him. Or would she? Yes, she would. He thought she was irresistible, which was a long way from the truth, and he must have talked about her as though she was Scarlett O'Hara. She said, 'Don't believe it. I don't know what he said, but don't believe it.'

She didn't want to know. She was sure she would find it embarrassing, and she wished passionately that Uncle Ted had kept his mouth shut.

'Not even that you came down here to escape the latest who wants to marry you?'

'Uncle Ted,' she said solemnly into the night ahead, 'when I get home I shall poison your malted milk. And why on earth should you and my uncle be discussing me?'

'You're his favourite subject.'

'Well, that must have been terribly boring for you. I do apologise.'

'Don't apologise, it wasn't boring at all.' It was all very well to joke about it, but it was embarrassing. She said,

'The real reason I came down here was because I was worried about him. I still am.' There was no response. He didn't even ask what she meant.

She turned her head, wondering if she should ask him outright about the business. She was used to driving this car and in this unaccustomed seat the side of the road seemed too close so that she frowned and tensed for a moment. Then she adjusted to the situation and looked back at Leon. 'I didn't know the crafts shop was lease-hold,' she was going to say, but he spoke first.

'There's no need for you to worry,' he said.

Later she felt that she might have asked some questions, instead of accepting that as the answer to them all, but for the moment she was reassured.

The Plover was a typical Cotswold hotel, set in lonely lovely countryside. It had once been a manor farm and it was run by three generations of the same family, all plump and well-fed and glowing, who welcomed Leon with broad smiles.

While Fran was phoning Uncle Ted Leon and mine host were chatting over the menu, and Fran wondered who had come with him last time. Judith perhaps? As Uncle Ted had told Leon so much about Fran maybe Uncle Ted could tell Fran rather more about Leon. Such as the story of Judith.

But right now she said, 'We're having supper just outside Chipping Campden. Don't wait up for me, I do have my key. Are you all right?'

Uncle Ted said he was just going to bed anyway, and of course he was all right.

She enjoyed herself very much. Articulate, cultivated and worldly, Leon made a superb companion, and she gave herself up to his charm, savouring the company like the food. Although he smiled rarely he could be very funny indeed. He had her gurgling with laughter, alight with it. And chattering nineteen to the dozen herself, so that it was a fairly riotous meal.

When they came out, to drive back home again, Poppy protested a little before she started, but no more than usual and Fran had no qualms. She snuggled down in her seat and said, 'Nobody but me has driven this car since I had it. Is that an honour for you?'

'I appreciate it,' said Leon. 'You can drive my car some time.'

'Me at the wheel, you in the passenger seat?'

'I'll try to overcome my prejudices for a short trip.'

'You should,' she said impulsively. 'I've overcome mine.'

He knew what she meant, and she thought—I really have. I like you now. I'm not being added to any collection, but if we stop on the way home I wouldn't mind a goodnight kiss. She pushed back her hair with both hands as though she felt other fingers against her temples, and pushed away the thought of Judith in Leon's arms at the same time.

Poppy sighed and stopped. They were going downhill at the time. As the impetus ended Fran realised that the engine was silent, and slowly they came to a halt. 'Oh no!' she gasped.

'Petrol?' She pointed to the fuel gauge, still registering a couple of gallons. 'Does that work?' he asked.

'Of course it does.'

'Well, something doesn't. You steer while I get it on to the verge.'

The verges and hedgerows were sodden with rain, a heavy vehicle would have sunk in and got bogged down, but Poppy was lightweight and it would be more than risky to stay on the narrow lane on such a dark night. It was late and you couldn't guarantee that a car or a lorry wouldn't come hurtling down that hill.

Fran moved behind the wheel while Leon went to the back and shoved, and Poppy bumped over the rough grass, stopping just short of the ditch as Fran put on the brakes.

They weren't far from the hotel. They'd have to go

back there and phone for help. If only it would stop drizzling. If the moon had been out and a few stars, and if it had been dry underfoot, this could have been an amusing end to the evening instead of a wretched nuisance.

She got out, her heels making little sucking sounds in the spongy turf as she walked round to the front of the car, where Leon had the bonnet up. She said, 'It makes a change, doesn't it, the girl's car breaking down?'

He grunted, 'Got a torch?'

She went to the side compartment and fished around for the flat pocket torch that she was almost sure was there. She hadn't used her own car after dark for ages, she wished she hadn't tonight, and when she did find the torch and switched it on the beam was so pale it was almost invisible.

'This isn't going to be much use,' she said. It crawled over the engine like a glowworm, and she ventured, 'What are you looking for?'

'Damned if I know,' he said. 'Do you know anything about engines?'

'I read the book once, it's in the car. But I just take it into the garage, and it's never done this before.'

'I notice you've stopped calling it "she".'

'Poor Poppy. Do you think it's serious?'

'Let's get back,' he said, 'before they put up the shutters at the Plover.'

It seemed to be uphill all the way, and she wouldn't have blamed him if he'd blamed her. If it had been his car she wouldn't have been in the sunniest of moods herself, but as Poppy's owner she was responsible for their plight. She said, 'I'm sorry about this,' when they were half way up the first hill, and he grinned.

'Cheer up. They'll put another log on the fire for us

and we'll get help for Poppy as soon as the first garage opens.'

He put an arm around her and they strode on, the thought of the big open fire ahead getting more tempting every minute. There had been some nice deep armchairs. She could curl up comfortably in one of them and wait till morning. Or take a room. It was residential and they had seemed very nice, very pleased to see Leon. Fran was sure they would do their best to find a couple of rooms.

One lorry passed them. When they saw its lights coming they scrambled on to the verge and she found herself huddled against Leon. In spite of the cold and drizzle that was very comforting. She smiled up at him, 'This isn't going to do your velvet jacket much good.'

'How's the homespun skirt?' he said.

'Shrinking, I think.'

He helped her back on to the road; her long skirt wasn't ideal for walking through the rainy night and by the time they reached the hotel she was out of breath. She sat on a white bench near the closed front door, puffing, while Leon went round the back. There were lights still on, upstairs and down, and in a very short time the front door opened and Fran, damp and dishevelled, was ushered in and taken to the fire, with as much fuss as though she had been in a real accident instead of a simple breakdown.

The fire was still burning brightly, and she sat in front of it, sipping a hot drink that was put into her hand, while Leon was talking to the proprietor.

A girl of about Fran's age, the owner's daughter, came and sat beside her and talked about the weather, 'Isn't it foul?' and how the best of cars could sometimes break down. 'He's got a TR 7, hasn't he?'

'Not tonight,' said Fran. 'We came in my ancient Mini.

All the same, I never had any trouble with her before.'

'That is a pretty skirt,' said the girl suddenly. 'I admired it when you first came in.'

Fran delved into her handbag. 'I got it from the shop where I work.' She found one of the crafts shop cards and Leon, who had been on the phone, came over as she handed it to the girl.

'Touting for trade,' said Fran, smiling.

'Ted will be proud of you,' said Leon. 'There's a taxi coming.'

A taxi, of course. How odd that she hadn't thought of such an obvious solution. It was Leon saying that about getting help for Poppy as soon as the first garage opened. She had thought they would be waiting till then and she felt deflated, as though she had missed out on a small treat.

'We could easily have put you up,' the girl said, and Fran knew they had suggested that to Leon who had turned down the offer. Getting a taxi to get them home tonight was very sensible, but it would have been pleasant to have sat by the fire here a little longer and then gone up to a pretty bedroom and got out of her wet clothes. She wasn't worried about her morning face. She knew that, for a change, she could look quite fetching shining clean, and she did have a lipstick in her handbag.

The taxi took some time. Fran's skirt steamed and her eyelids grew heavy. This had been a long day, and if anyone had asked for her opinion she would have preferred to stay overnight and order the taxi for early in the morning.

When the girl left them Fran said, 'They were offering us two rooms, of course?'

'Of course.'

'Why didn't we take them?' She yawned. 'If that

taxi's much longer I'll be asleep anyway, not to mention a candidate for pneumonia.'

'Give it another ten minutes. I'd rather get you home tonight.' He smiled his rare smile. 'I imagine that Ted could be rather an old-fashioned guardian.'

'I did phone him.' Once you start yawning it's hard to stop, she was still yawning as she spoke. 'He won't wake till breakfast time.' She closed her eyes. 'And he's not my guardian. I'm not an old-fashioned girl. I please myself where I spend my nights.'

She had a few quiet moments after that. In the dining room they had finished laying the tables for breakfast when she opened her eyes, and Leon was sitting watching her.

She suddenly realised that what she had just said might be misunderstood. She should have thought before she spoke, but she was tired and not feeling over-bright.

There was a knock on the door and she was quite relieved to see the taxi driver. Some men might have interpreted that bit about spending her nights as she pleased as a come-on, and Leon Aldridge was both cynical and sophisticated. It could have been awkward trying to explain to him that Fran, in her heart of hearts, was an old-fashioned girl after all.

# CHAPTER FIVE

POPPY was a shadow beneath the hedgerows in the beam of the taxi lights, and Fran said dolefully, 'She looks abandoned. I hope no one will think she's been dumped.'

'She isn't that decrepit.' Leon pulled Fran's head on to his shoulder. 'You can close your eyes again,' he said. 'I'll let you know when we get there.'

She did close her eyes. She lay against Leon, his arm around her, and thought about nothing at all because she fell asleep and only woke when the taxi stopped.

'You're home,' he said.

'So I am. Heavens! Sorry.'

'Sorry for what?'

'Falling asleep. Not very polite, was it?'

'It's been a long night.'

The taxi was parked in the road just outside the Galleries. Leon paid the fare, and as the taxi drove away they walked across the flagstoned frontage to the crafts shop door. 'A longer night than I expected,' said Fran, 'with plenty of variety.'

She found her key and opened the door and said, 'Thank you and goodnight,' reaching up and brushing his cheek lightly with her lips. She expected him to take her into his arms and kiss her properly, but instead he said, 'Thank you. I'm away until Thursday, may I come round in the evening?'

'Yes, of course. We'll be glad to see you.' She stepped inside and he went towards the back of the house and his car. Fran turned on a light and walked quietly and carefully between counters and displays. At the top of the stairs, as she turned off the shop light, she heard the soft powerful purr of his car engine and stood listening until it faded. It was well past midnight. She would have to get up early and phone a garage and wash her hair, but the cat-nap in the taxi had refreshed her and cleared her mind.

She tiptoed into the bathroom, she didn't want to wake Uncle Ted, and got out of her muddy shoes and damp skirt. Then, as she was shivering a little and it would be stupid to risk catching a cold, she risked running the hot water and hoped the cistern wouldn't make too much noise.

It *had* been a long and varied night. She had enjoyed most of it very much. She had enjoyed being with Leon, and when she had brushed his cheek with her lips just now a strange tingle had run up and down her spine. She would have liked him to hold her tighter. She was trying to disturb him a little, so that his self-control was a little at risk. It was like driving the car, a small struggle for power. Fran was used to being the one in charge, and Leon was a challenge like Everest, almost impossible to conquer but very exhilarating to try.

She was washing her hair at the sink, where she could keep an eye on the breakfast cooking at the same time, when Uncle Ted came down next morning. He blinked at her and she said, 'I got my hair soaked last night. The car broke down.'

'Oh dear!'

'Could you pour yourself a cup of tea? I've just made it. It was my car, I'll have to start looking up garages in a minute. We came back by taxi.'

He poured his tea and she began to towel her hair. After he had taken a few sips he said, 'I'm sorry about that. Did you have a good time, until the car broke down?'

'A very good time.'

'I knew you would,' he said smugly.

'Don't rush it. Think what my mother would say if she heard who took me to the theatre last night.'

He winced at that. Although Fran was teasing they both knew there was no way in which Isabel would be reconciled to the idea of Ted, much less Fran, becoming friendly with Leon. If she found out there would be ugly trouble.

Maybe she need never know. She wouldn't come down here, so part of Fran's life would always be a closed book to her. If the relationship ever became serious then Fran would have to confide in Jim, and they'd have to go about breaking the news very gently indeed.

But that was leaping much too far ahead, and Fran was astonished to find herself thinking that way. 'We met a Judith Waring at the theatre,' she said. 'She knew Leon *very* well. He says she's a designer—do you know her?'

'Not really,' said Uncle Ted. 'Except that she's Sholto Wallpapers.'

Wallpapers and furnishing fabrics for the better homes. 'She works for a classy firm,' said Fran, turning her attention back to the stove and dishing up Uncle Ted's sausage and tomatoes.

He was eating his cooked breakfast without protest these days, he was eating all his meals. He picked up his knife and fork and added, 'Her father owns the firm,' and Fran gave a derisive chortle.

'Well, that should give her a flying start.'

Of course she was being unfair. Judith Waring could be a brilliant designer, but if she was, as well as looking exquisite and being the boss's daughter, then that proved yet again that it was an unfair world.

Uncle Ted said, 'Leon's a popular young man——'

'And there are bound to be Judiths around,' Fran finished it for him. She sat down, reaching for her own half-cold cup of tea. 'And talking about colourful pasts, what *have* you been telling him about me?'

'Not much,' said Uncle Ted. He'd talked about Fran, but he wasn't admitting that he'd embroidered on anything.

'Not even about Arthur?' Fran persisted. 'Sure you didn't tell Leon I dashed down here because Arthur was going crazy over me.'

'Indeed I did not,' said Uncle Ted with dignity. 'But you did want to get away because Mr Deane was becoming pertinacious, didn't you?'

'If that means a nuisance,' said Fran, 'I suppose so.'

'I told him you were a popular young lady,' said Uncle Ted, as if that pleased him.

'That makes us a popular pair,' said Fran lightly. But however Uncle Ted looked at it Judith Waring obviously had far more in common with Leon than Fran had.

Gerald told her that, bluntly, later in the morning. He came in at eleven o'clock and asked, 'Any coffee going?'

'Sure,' said Fran. This was the time she made coffee, which they drank in the office with the door open so that they could see if any customers came into the shop. Uncle Ted was showing someone paperweights, and Fran had just walked to the door with a customer who had bought a rag doll dressed as Henry the Eighth.

Now she went into the office and switched on the electric kettle, dropping coffee bags into three yellow mugs. She hoped that Gerald wasn't going to take up where he had left off when the roses came, and as he sat down in Uncle Ted's chair behind the desk she was

93

reminded of Arthur cross-questioning her on evenings she had spent away from him.

The two men didn't look at all alike, except in an expression of suspicious sulkiness, which Gerald was doing his best to hide under a jaunty manner. 'Enjoy yourself last night?' he asked.

'Who told you?'

Leon might have done, or one of the customers who was in the shop when Leon came in. Or someone who had seen them at the theatre or in the Plover. Gerald said, 'News gets around,' and Fran shrugged,

'It was no secret.'

'I'm not saying it was. I'm only asking if you enjoyed yourself.'

'Yes, thank you.' She produced the half bottle of milk and the packet of sugar. 'Until the car broke down,' she said, and Gerald goggled.

'That doesn't sound like Leon's car. Nor like Leon.'

'My car.'

'Where did you go in your car?'

'Somewhere to eat?'

'Where?' he snapped, and she snapped back,

'Is that your concern?'

He had to admit that it wasn't, and then he grinned ruefully, 'Except that I saw you first!'

Gerald couldn't be serious about her, their dates had been completely casual, but it might be a knock to his pride if she started going around with his boss, and he would have to put an affable face on it because he couldn't afford to rile Leon. That must be frustrating for him.

I wish you didn't work next door, Fran thought. This makes a difficult situation. She also wished she could say, 'We're just friends, aren't we, all of us?' But she knew that she would rather go around with Leon than any other man. She didn't want Gerald saying, 'When will you come out with me?'

The kettle boiled and she made the coffee and Gerald said, 'Well, I'll be around.'

'There's always a cup of coffee.' She smiled and handed it to him, milked and sugared, and he gulped down a little as though it was bitter aloes.

'Funny,' he said, 'when you said you didn't like Leon I was pleading his cause. It might have been better if I'd given you a few more reasons for feeling that way.'

'What reasons?' she demanded instinctively.

After a second or two he said, 'The girl he's going to marry for one. Her name's Judith, and her old man is Sholto Wallpapers.'

'I met her last night,' said Fran with studied casualness. 'But nobody said anything about a wedding.'

'Others come and go,' Gerald insisted, 'but Judith Waring is going to end up as Leon's wife.'

'Does he know?'

'Of course he knows.'

'I'm sure they'll be very happy,' said Fran flippantly. There was no marriage understanding between them yet, or Judith would not have walked away and left Fran and Leon together last night. But they had looked as well matched as though a computer had selected them as the perfect couple. Fran could understand why friends took it for granted that they would eventually pair off permanently.

She perched on the side of the desk and sipped her own coffee, then asked, 'Anything else?'

'Er—no,' said Gerald, taking his time drawling that out, and she marked his hesitation again. Earlier he had paused over what he should say, and Fran had the feeling that he could have told her about something worse than Judith Waring.

She bit her lip, torn between curiosity and caution, and then decided that she shouldn't be prying like this. It was underhand, gossiping about a friend. Gerald had become almost as biased as she used to be, anything he said against Leon right now was open to doubt. Anyhow she didn't think she wanted to hear. She said,

'I wonder if Uncle Ted's ready for his coffee,' and opened the door to look through into the shop.

He was just completing his sale, counting out change. There were several other people looking around, and she gulped down her cup of coffee as fast as she could. 'Excuse me,' she said. 'Business is booming. It's all go, isn't it?'

'Don't you wish it was?' said Gerald.

'Have a heart,' she smiled, 'it isn't that bad. We're keeping our heads above water.'

'Are you?' He looked as though he doubted it, and she was glad to get away from him. Fran touched her uncle's shoulder and told him,

'There's a cup of coffee in there for you.' Then she hovered until she could move in to chat up a customer, pointing out that the samplers were handstitched, copies of Victorian samplers but heirlooms of the future.

She was getting a real kick from her job. Her delight and her enthusiasm were infectious, and nearly always customers went out pleased with their purchases and smiling.

As Gerald left he gave her a wry grin and a wave, and thought what a knock-out she looked. She was wearing jeans and a pink cheesecloth shirt that showed an inch of midriff when she stretched for a high shelf. She was a nice girl, but no match for Leon, any more than poor old Ted was.

It's a damn shame, thought Gerald, going back into the Galleries and shutting himself in the room marked 'Manager'.

Leon was in London for the next three days or Gerald might not have slipped round next door. He had always had a high regard and a healthy respect for Leon Aldridge. Gerald would not have cared to stand up against his employer, and that wasn't just because of the job either.

He wished he could have warned Fran how things stood, because he liked her and it *was* a damn shame, but as Fran had said, it wasn't his concern. He clenched his hands into impotent fists, because he couldn't do a flaming thing, except grin and bear it and get on with his work...

Fran was looking forward to Thursday and seeing Leon again. Tuesday and Wednesday evenings she spent happily at home with Uncle Ted. There was plenty to do, both in the flat and the shop. Once she was confident about running the shop on her own she would pack Uncle Ted off for that rest he needed, a week or two by the sea maybe, maybe at the boarding house at Brighton.

She darned a couple of pullovers for him—he had always disliked new clothes—answered a few letters and phoned the farm to reassure her mother that all was well. When Fran said how much she was enjoying being here Isabel asked after Gerald.

The last time Fran had phoned she had talked about Gerald, and her mother supposed she was still going around with him. An eligible young man would be some consolation prize to her mother, even if it did mean Fran staying in Stratford. 'He's very well,' Fran had said.

'Have you been out anywhere?' her mother asked, and Fran admitted,

'I've been to the theatre.'

Shakespeare wasn't her mother's cup of tea, and if she had asked 'Who with?' Fran would probably have fibbed, 'Several folk. Nobody special.' But her mother wasn't interested in discussing the play and she took it for granted that Fran's escort had been Gerald. Fran came away from the telephone wondering how long she could keep Leon's name out of her phone calls. She'd have to talk to Jim before there was any mention of Leon Aldridge to her mother.

On Thursday Fran woke up feeling excited. She couldn't think why for a moment or two. She just opened her eyes feeling marvellous, and stretched her arms high above her head, yawning luxuriously. The sky was grey, glimpsed through her window, but it was going to be a lovely day, and of *course* she was seeing Leon again this evening.

She got up, singing softly, and as the day wore on she realised that she never counted the hours before. Since she was seventeen or eighteen there had always been a man in her life, and she had looked forward to her dates with varying degrees of pleasurable anticipation. But she had never clock-watched, keeping tags on time and feeling excitement build up inside her until she had difficulty in keeping still. She wanted to dance around, and it didn't really matter if she did.

She had always been quick-moving, a little restless. The customers saw a lithe and lively girl, with a smile that could have sold a lawnmower to someone in a high-rise flat. Business was brisk and Uncle Ted was surprised when six o'clock struck.

'A very good day,' he pronounced it, checking the till.

They closed the door and Fran ran upstairs. She had braised steak for the evening meal, and she had no idea what time Leon would be calling, nor what they would do when he did.

It had been an haphazard arrangement ... 'May I come round on Thursday evening?' 'Yes, of course, we'll be glad to see you.'

But during the last three days she had had time to appreciate the impression that Leon Aldridge had made on her. She had thought about him constantly, lingering in her mind on the way he had looked and acted, the things he had said, as she had never done with any man before. She was eager to reach the next stage of getting to know each other, learning a little more, coming a little closer.

She cleansed her face of the day's dust and grime as fast as she could, then got into another pair of jeans and a yellow and white checked shirt. She was tempted to wear something prettier, but she didn't want to appear dressed up for an occasion. This was how she would have been for another evening with Uncle Ted, comfortable and casual.

It was bad enough to have her heart palpitating without dressing to match. Leon was calling round, as he had apparently often dropped in on Uncle Ted, and it would be idiotic to show herself more than friendly and neighbourly.

Uncle Ted knew he was coming. As they ate their meal he asked, not for the first time, 'Do you suppose Leon will have eaten before he arrives?'

'I have no idea,' said Fran, yet again. She hadn't saved any steak, but she could find food if food was needed. They talked about the day's happenings and Uncle Ted was unaware she was on tenterhooks, listening for the doorbell all the time.

She tried to concentrate on what she was eating and what was being said, but the undercurrent of excitement kept her from relaxing. If he doesn't come after all, she thought, I'm going to feel like a wet rag by bedtime.

She tried to laugh at herself; this was silly, but it was quite pleasant too, racing and heady as though her blood was sparkling. She had always had energy, always felt alive, but tonight she was on tiptoe with excitement.

Leon didn't ring the doorbell, he knocked on the communicating door at the end of the passage, and Fran said, 'I hope this isn't Gerald.'

'Unlikely at this hour,' said Uncle Ted. It was nearly eight o'clock.

She got up and walked along the passage very calmly. And all the time she was thinking, I never felt this way before. Some girls always do, every new man they date sends their pulses racing, every one is the right one for a while. But I never before walked towards a door and knew that the person I most wanted to see was standing there, waiting for the door to open.

She fumbled with the bolts because her hands were shaking, although she steadied them before she lifted the latch and smiled a nice natural friendly welcome.

He stood looking at her, then he smiled too and said, 'Hello.'

'We've been waiting for you.'

'I'd like that.' Fran wasn't sure what he meant, but it sounded right, and when he stepped through the door they brushed against each other, shoulders, hands, and somehow she was in his arms and he was kissing her gently. Or perhaps it was casually, because almost at once they were walking down the passage and he was asking if Poppy was back on the road.

'It was only a fuel blockage,' she said. 'The garage told me that if I'd put my foot down on the accelerator and blasted away I might have cleared it.'

'We'll remember next time.'

'Had a good business trip?' she asked.

'Pretty good. How's business been for you?'

'Pretty good. Especially today.'

Uncle Ted beamed on them as they came into the room, and that evening Fran sat curled on the settee and tried to decide how much of Leon's charisma was sex appeal, and how much was intellectual. He had a first-class mind. If she had shut her eyes and listened she would still have been impressed and attracted. But when you looked at him you saw that, even sitting in one of those funny little wickerwork armchairs, he was sensuous as a panther, his lithe body smooth hard muscle.

He sat still, with no wasted movements, and Fran tried to ration her own gestures. But it was against nature for her, and almost impossible for her to talk with an expressionless face and motionless hands.

He was self-contained, an introvert, her opposite, and she knew what they said about opposites always attracting. She had never really believed it before, but now she was hoping it was true because she was very attracted to Leon.

He had to be interested in her because one date followed another in the next few weeks. They weren't exactly inseparable, but she couldn't see how he could be dating any other girl, she was sure she was around for most of his free time. Besides, when they came upon friends of his she thought she could read from their faces that she wasn't one of the collection. They looked hard at her, weighing her up, as though she was someone to be reckoned with, and although they might have been comparing her with Judith nobody said anything that might have been embarrassing.

After that first night at the theatre they didn't come across Judith again. Leon had a wide circle of friends, or acquaintances. Women's eyes lit up when they saw him and men came eagerly over, but Fran soon realised that he was a loner. Whether they were with a crowd, or talking to each other, she felt instinctively that he held back, keeping secrets.

But he was enormously exciting to be near. Physically she was infatuated, she supposed. She fancied him more than any other man she had met so far. That might have been because their lovemaking was still at the uncommitted stage, but a slight contact like his fingers closing over hers could make her nerves sing out in a fierce and delicate pain. When they danced one evening she felt drugged with pleasure, and kisses were moments of mindless delight.

She could be heading for a very passionate affair, something very serious. But in the meantime she reported in her weekly phone calls back to the farm that she was not going around with Gerald any more. She was into a group now. That was partly true, she had met other men and women through Leon, and the artists who stocked the crafts shop were all friendly.

Her mother wasn't sure about this. Arthur had been up to the farm to complain that he was getting no replies to his letters and to ask for Fran's phone number. Arthur had phoned Fran that night and got Uncle Ted who had told him she was out with friends.

'I've written to Arthur,' Fran told her mother now. 'I wished him the best of luck and told him not to keep the job open.' He had mentioned the job in both his letters, and that the girls who turned up to be interviewed weren't up to Fran's shorthand and typing speeds.

'But if Gerald isn't asking you out any more,' her mother said plaintively, 'perhaps you shouldn't be too hasty about Arthur. He has a good steady business, you know.'

'So have I,' said Fran. 'And I don't love Arthur.'

She heard her mother's sigh. 'Love isn't everything,' said Isabel tremulously. 'You can't live on love.'

'True,' said Fran. It was no good arguing, no use telling her mother that marriage was no longer considered as a meal ticket for life. Fran wanted love. Any permanent relationship she formed would be based on love, and so far she wasn't in love with anybody. But she was powerfully attracted to Leon, and it wouldn't take much to tip that awareness of him into loving.

If he stopped holding back, showed himself to be vulnerable and less self-sufficient, then she was almost sure that she would find she was beginning to love him.

She didn't see very much of Gerald. He didn't come in for coffee now. When she was out at the front of the crafts shop he sometimes joined her and they exchanged a few words.

'You're getting prettier,' he'd said the last time, and she'd laughed.

'The climate must suit me.' It was another dull day, but everything around here did suit her. She had taken to this way of life so well that she could hardly believe she was only into her fifth week. At the beginning there had been that idea that she should come down for a month and see how things went, but even her mother had realised by now that this was no holiday.

Business wasn't booming, but customers were coming

in a steady stream, and Uncle Ted was leaving her to do more and more of the selling.

In the Galleries an exhibition was running, the artist whose work Leon had shown Fran that first Sunday, and she meant to have a look before it closed. There was a notice by the front door of the Galleries, 'Exhibition of paintings by Florence Pizer', a housewife who had found she could paint when the children grew up and left home.

During a slack spell one afternoon, after Fran had been arranging some of her small wares outside on a polished elm table, she wandered into the Galleries.

Everything in here was on display, with space around it. The crafts shop customers rooted among the merchandise, but in the Galleries they stood back to survey, only rarely handling some of the sculptures.

A young man assistant, who knew Fran of course, stepped forward and she smiled. 'Just looking,' she said. The exhibition was signposted and filled a couple of adjoining alcoves on the ground floor, and several of the paintings had a little red 'sold' sticker in the corner. Good for Florence, thought Fran. Leon had said she was selling fairly well.

Another man and a woman were walking around, and Fran stood for a while in front of the painting of a young cat, tiger-eyed in a face as pretty as a pansy. I'd like that, she thought. I might buy that.

She jumped as Gerald touched her shoulder. 'You startled me. Isn't that pretty?'

'Yes,' he said. 'Looking for Leon?'

'Looking at the pictures.'

'Because he isn't here. He won't be in until tomorrow.'

'I know he won't,' she said.

She walked on with Gerald, talking about the paintings, and the painter who had waited until half her life was over before she had seriously put brush to canvas. 'She joined an art club for a hobby,' said Gerald, 'and discovered she had talent, as simple as that.'

It was a serene and gentle talent. Perhaps that was why it had never upset the tenor of her life. Fran said quietly, 'I wish my father had never known he was an artist.'

'Do you?'

His talent had surpassed this woman's, Fran was sure, but it had given him no peace. 'If he hadn't felt that he had to paint he'd never have gone away and he probably wouldn't have died,' she said. 'He might have been a genius, but I'd rather he'd been happy.'

'You're happy, aren't you?' The question caught her unaware. Gerald's spectacles gave him an owlish expression when he was being earnest. He blinked behind them now and Fran blinked too.

'Yes,' she said, honestly, 'I am very happy.'

'Yes, I thought so.' They were in the main centre of the Galleries now, still dominated by the massive rock statue. 'Look,' said Gerald, 'how about you having a coffee with me this morning? I owe you a few cups and I'm about due for one.'

'I'd better get back.'

'Surely your uncle can manage without you for ten minutes?'

She was going to say he couldn't, but that was nonsense, and it was rather bad manners refusing. 'Thanks,' she said, 'I'll look in and see how he's coping.'

Of course he was coping, and she went back and went with Gerald into his office. The last time she had been in here, the only time, was the morning after she broke the vase.

'I see you've got another vase up there,' she said. 'Is it another fake?'

'Yes.'

Leon had said, 'Send something to a charity,' and she had made a donation to a local village church roof in memory of the vase. She laughed now. 'I still get nightmares about that.' She didn't of course, she was joking.

A young man brought in a tray with two cups of coffee and grinned at her, and began to say something about the Florence Pizer paintings when Gerald cut in, 'Thank you,' pointedly dismissing him.

Fran stared. Gerald sounded very unsociable, as though this was going to be a difficult interview rather than a neighbourly cup of coffee. He hadn't smiled when she'd laughed, and he wasn't smiling now.

She took her cup and helped herself to milk and sugar. Then she said, 'You look as though something rather unpleasant has turned up. I hope it's not me.'

He still didn't smile. He was sitting with his cup before him and he frowned down into it, then he looked up still frowning and said jerkily, 'We're friends, aren't we?'

'Yes?' Yes, they were, and why was he asking the question?

'You know what I told you about Judith?'

'Yes?' The same intonation came out.

'Nothing's changed,' said Gerald abruptly, and after a few seconds of silence Fran said,

'I'm not following you. Let's take it slowly. You say that Leon and Judith are going to marry?'

Gerald looked hot and bothered. He ran a finger round his collar as though it had become tight. 'Some time, yes,' he said.

'Then she's very broadminded,' said Fran gently, 'because he's been spending a fair amount of time with me these last weeks.'

'I know that.' He gulped and blurted, 'And I know why.'

'Do tell me.' He was going to tell her, so she might as well take it calmly. She wasn't worried, but she wished she hadn't said all right to this cup of coffee.

'He likes you, of course,' said Gerald. 'You're a real girl, going around with you is no hardship.' Fran's lips twitched, and she wondered if she should say, 'Thank you.' 'But it's business really,' said Gerald.

'Business?'

Gerald leaned forward, narrowly missing his coffee cup. 'He wants to take over the crafts shop. He wants your uncle's signature on a few more papers.'

She said quickly, 'Why? He owns the whole building. Our bit's leasehold.'

'Leases aren't what they used to be,' Gerald sounded grim. 'There's no chucking the tenants out into the street these days. Besides, there are still a few more years to run, and he wants the place now.'

'What for?'

'To enlarge the Galleries, I suppose.'

Uncle Ted had talked about Leon helping the crafts shop carry on, not closing it down. Gerald only 'supposed' Leon wanted to enlarge the Galleries, so he didn't really know. This could be a storm in a teacup, and Fran asked bluntly, 'Why are you telling me this?'

'Because I like you,' said Gerald.

'Thanks,' she muttered ironically, and he went on as though he hadn't heard her.

'It would be a fair business offer, Leon wouldn't do old Ted down as far as money went, and it's legitimate tactics to get you on his side as well. But you're taking it personally, and Leon isn't.'

And how did he know that? She couldn't imagine Leon discussing her with Gerald. Leon was the last man to go into any details about his private life with anyone.

'He's the coolest customer I've ever known,' said Gerald. 'He's——' He hesitated, and because what he had just said was exactly how Fran had thought of Leon for years she murmured,

'Ice? An iceman?'

'What?' Gerald considered that, then nodded. 'Yes. Yes, in some ways you could say that.' He went on with complete sincerity, 'There's no man alive I've got more respect for. He's a great bloke. If I was in trouble he'd help me out in any way he could. But I wouldn't go to him for sympathy. I wouldn't expect any sympathy from him. I don't think he could shed tears for anybody, not even for himself. In all the years I've known him I've never seen him lose his head or do anything that wasn't calculated. He's cool. He's always cool.'

Gerald had worked with Leon for a long time, he should know something about him, and he was telling Fran now that Leon was cold and without pity. When she first came here she would have agreed wholeheartedly, but not now. *No*, she thought.

'Women go for him, Fran,' said Gerald mournfully. 'I don't need to tell you that.' He floundered. 'I mean, they would, wouldn't they? He's got what it takes, what they want.' Fran had said nothing for some time, and Gerald said in a final burst, 'Some of them have made proper Charlies of themselves, but he always knows where he's going, every inch of the way.'

That was all he had to say. He looked thoroughly

miserable, sitting hunched in his chair, his untouched coffee in front of him.

'Can I ask him about taking over the shop?' asked Fran, and saw Gerald gulp again.

'You can,' he said huskily. 'I suppose you will, and he isn't going to thank me for telling you.' Gerald had acted impulsively and was beginning to regret it. 'I suppose you couldn't ask your uncle, could you?' he suggested. 'Get round it, and leave me out of it?'

'I could do that,' said Fran. Of course she would be asking her uncle, and there was no need to tell anyone about Gerald's indiscretions. She didn't want to cause trouble for him. He could even find himself out of a job and he could hardly claim wrongful dismissal if he had been broadcasting business secrets.

But she didn't have to ask Uncle Ted because, just before closing time, a man came in who produced some of their best selling pottery lines, and he and Uncle Ted were talking ahead. From the way Uncle Ted was acting he didn't foresee the crafts shop closing down.

The potter had a selection of new designs and when Fran went into the office they were discussing next year's market. She was asked for her opinion and chose some attractive little porringers as a likely winner, and Uncle Ted gave an order for delivery in the autumn.

Later, over their evening meal, she told him about the paintings in the exhibition. 'They're not very expensive,' she said, 'and there's one of a cat I might buy. I'm thinking about it. You might go in and have a look at it and tell me what you think.'

Uncle Ted said he would, pleased she was asking his advice.

'It seems awfully big next door,' she said, stirring her

soup thoughtfully. 'They're hardly cramped for space, are they?'

'Hardly,' Uncle Ted agreed.

'Perhaps they could spare us a bit more,' Fran smiled. 'We're the ones with the piled-up merchandise.'

He chuckled. 'I think they need all they've got. I think Leon considers the present boundary a fair division.'

She was reassured then that there was no question of enlarging the Galleries by annexing the crafts shop. If that had ever been mentioned Uncle Ted would not have been joking so cheerfully now. So Gerald was wrong.

She didn't believe he had lied to her deliberately. He thought he was right, and he thought he knew Leon. He did know Leon of course, up to a point, but Fran imagined she was a little beyond that point.

She wished she could have told Gerald, 'I know Leon better than anyone else does. He isn't always cool and calculating, and the reasons he spends time with me are not business reasons.'

They were the usual man—woman reasons. Because he enjoyed her company and he found her attractive. He didn't want the crafts shop, but she was fairly sure that he wanted her. She knew from the way he looked at her, touched her.

The control was always there, but three weeks wasn't long, and they had never been quite alone, except in a car, since that first meal here in this room. They had always gone out and about.

Tomorrow night, she thought; and Uncle Ted asked, 'Why aren't you eating your soup?'

He had finished his, and she began to eat. 'Still wondering about that picture,' she said.

Tomorrow night they would be at Leon's house. She hadn't been there before, but they were having a meal there and they would be alone. She supposed they would be alone, and she supposed he would want to make love to her.

When that happened she knew that she could keep her head because she always had, and Leon was too sophisticated to force an issue or let a scene get out of hand. She had expected an exciting but civilised evening.

But, after listening to Gerald, she was filled with an almost primitive desire to know that Leon could be shaken out of his self-control if it was only for a moment.

Perhaps it was to prove to herself that she was not one of the crowd, but she wanted him to admit that he wanted her terribly, and to hear him say—as though it meant more than it had ever meant when he'd said it before—'I want *you* . . . I love *you* . . .'

ONCE she had made up her mind what was going to happen tomorrow evening Fran's spirits became buoyant
again. She had been a little depressed since her interview
with Gerald. It hadn't shown, but she had been left with
a slight uneasiness.

She knew that Leon liked her, that that was why he
never left her without fixing their next meeting. She had
always said, 'Yes, I'll come,' because that was what she
wanted to say. And so, presumably, had the girls who
had made 'proper Charlies' of themselves, according to
Gerald.

If she began to play hard to get, and changed her mind
about tomorrow evening, that might make Leon realise
how much he had counted on her company. Or it could
simply make him decide that she was inconsiderate.
Anyhow, Fran wasn't made for the waiting game, she
wasn't a calculator. She would find it much more enjoyable to flirt a little . . .

Getting ready, she dressed with especial care. She
always took pains with her appearance when she went
out on a date, but tonight she was making herself look as
irresistible as possible.

She had a gauzy dress she had bought and worn when
they went dancing. It had a scooped neckline, a sweeping skirt and sweeping sleeves, and it was in a myriad
shades of green, from pastel to deep blue-green, so that
when you moved it took on the shifting colours of the
sea. It was, she decided, her most romantic dress, and
some of the green matched her eyes.

She brushed her hair long and hard, until it fell into

deep waves, except for the occasional escaping tendril, and wore the tiny pearl earrings.

Dabbing perfume here and there she smiled at herself in the mirror, because who would have thought it—here she was dressing up to seduce a man, the huntress for the first time in her life. Not that she intended to seduce him all the way, she was a long way from a *femme fatale*. To lure, to entice, that was her aim, just to make him admit that she was special. Because he was. She hadn't told him yet, but tonight she would tell him.

'Very nice, my dear,' said Uncle Ted, just as her stepfather always said. Fran had had more than her share of unquestioning male devotion. The only real hurt she had ever known had been her father's silence during those last twelve months of his life.

Uncle Ted would have thought she looked very nice if she had been wearing a sack, but as she twirled around he practically gave her a round of applause. Then he said sharply, 'Mind the fire!' as the skirt flared out.

'It's flameproof,' she said. 'Non-combustible.'

'I like that dress,' said Leon, when he collected her.

'Me too,' she said gaily, 'that's why I'm in it.'

He laughed as though he was glad to see her, quiet laughter, and she realised all over again how attractive he was.

She knew there had been other girls, of course, there had been no need for Gerald to stress that. She had often wondered these last weeks, meeting women Leon knew —were you and he lovers? Were you ever the one beside him as I am now?

And Judith. They hadn't mentioned Judith again. Suppose she asked now, 'By the way, are you going to marry Judith Waring? And if you're not why does Gerald insist that you are?'

But she thought she knew the answer to that. 'Because Gerald has no idea. Because Gerald doesn't know.'

It was lovely in the car, close together and shut off from the world outside. Leon had been in Rome. Fran had been there once on a package holiday and they talked about Rome for a while. Then about the crafts shop, and she told him about the next-year stock Uncle Ted had just ordered, and he said nothing that could indicate there might not be a next year for the shop.

Of course there would, although she realised that she had been double checking.

She told him she had been into the Galleries to see the exhibition, but not that she had made up her mind to go in tomorrow and buy Florence Pizer's cat if it was still for sale. She wanted it for her bedroom wall, so that she could open her eyes in the morning and see those glowing eyes in that flower face.

The drive to Leon's house was along the bend of the river that was swollen and dark these days, flooding fields so that cattle and sheep had been moved on to higher ground, and creeping ominously near some of the riverside homes.

His garage, high on the river bank, had once housed a carriage and stabled horses. There were lights on in the flat above it, and Fran asked, 'Who lives there?'

'A couple who look after the house and garden.'

He didn't say their names, and it was beginning to rain again, which cut short her curiosity. They had to get down a path and over a bridge, and then through the trees and across to the house.

'Come on,' said Leon, and they ran. The bridge had iron railings and wooden slats, with the river flowing fast just below. Weeping willows edged the island, some of them half submerged, and then the path went through a little fringe of trees that effectively screened the house.

Once out of the trees the gardens were mainly lawns, with occasional shrubs and flower beds, very well kept, and right in the centre was the house.

It was a three-storey Edwardian house, big but not rambling. It looked more elegant and less fussy than most prosperous Edwardian homes, but Fran was intent on getting inside rather than inspecting the outside. She kept under the porch as Leon opened the front door with a key, and turned off a burglar alarm as he stepped inside.

The staircase wound up to the top floor. There was a grass green carpet in the hall and on the stairs, white walls and white paintwork except for bitter-chocolate gloss door frames.

A number of pictures were hanging. It was just coming up to dusk, and when he switched on lights she saw the details of the pictures. All the doors were closed and it was very quiet. She wiped her muddy shoes on a mat and asked, 'Anyone else here?'

He took her coat. 'I've no living-in staff these days. Do you mind?'

'No,' she said. 'But it's a big house for one.'

'It's a showplace. I sell as many pictures off the walls here as I do from the Gallery.' He looked around. 'Well, not quite, but that's what it is.'

Fran stopped herself saying, 'What a shame,' but it did seem rather a pity that this wasn't a home. It was certainly beautiful, with a combination of antique and modern.

The drawing room had Hepplewhite mirrors and chairs and a Persian carpet, as well as a modern sofa and easy chairs covered in natural linen, and glass-topped tables. The long window drapes took up the Persian carpet motif, and Fran wondered if they were a Sholto Wall-papers design, even Judith's own.

She could imagine Judith in this room, acting the gracious hostess. She wondered if Judith would mind if someone admired a painting on her walls and Leon promptly sold it to them.

It was warm, just the right temperature, and nowhere was there even a mark on a carpet or the suspicion of dust on the highly polished woodwork. Even the deep cushions on the sofa and chairs were plumped and free of wrinkles, and set smoothly in their place.

It was almost too perfect and she tried to stop think-ing about Judith, who must have been here dozens of times. And the others, whoever they were. She sipped a sherry in the drawing room while Leon made a phone call. He came back in about five minutes and said, 'Sorry about that. Business.'

'That's all right,' she said. She accepted it was business, but if it hadn't been she wouldn't have known. It had been a little eerie, sitting here by herself, imagining Judith's laughter, Judith talking to her guests. No doubt about it, this place would be the perfect setting for Judith.

The dining room was intimately small compared with the drawing room. A fire was burning in an Adam fire-place and the table was laid for two, even to unlit candles. The wallpaper looked like Sholto again, and the food was prepared and ready in a heated trolley.

Fran smiled, as Leon lit the candles and did the ser-ving. 'It's like one of those palaces in the fairy tales, where the traveller stumbles in from the storm and everything is waiting. All done by unseen hands.'

'It's always been a little like that,' said Leon.

There was jugged beef with a colourful assortment of

vegetables, and red wine. Then fruit and a cheese board. And in the candlelight and the firelight the meal was delicious and a lot of fun.

Fran found that she was doing most of the talking. Leon led her on to talk about her life in Yorkshire, so that she was telling him all sorts of things. Nothing hair-raising, nothing really spectacular had ever happened to her, but it had been happy and there had been things to laugh at, and good friends.

'But you're staying down here now?' he asked, and she thought he sounded a little anxious.

When she said, 'I think so,' he said,

'Good.'

'Is it?' She looked at him with wide green eyes and he smiled, and her heart flipped in that funny way it had begun to act lately, as she waited for him to tell her why he wanted her to stay. But instead he said,

'Shall we take the coffee into the drawing room?'

'That would be nice.'

They sat on the sofa with a coffee tray and two brandy glasses on a long glass-topped table in front of them, and went on talking. Softer now because they were very close. When he moved to fill a coffee cup he touched her and her skin sang out. When she breathed she felt that she could smell the smooth texture of his skin, the fair flopping hair, the warmth of his breath.

They were talking about one of the paintings on the wall, but in a desultory way because neither of them was looking at the painting. They were looking at each other, and Fran's throat was so dry that it ached.

'You're very beautiful,' said Leon, as she murmured something about perspective.

'So they tell me,' she croaked. She knew that she wasn't beautiful, although from time to time some man told her she was. But it had never affected her before so that she hardly knew what she was saying.

'I'm sure they do,' he said.

'So are you.' She spoke with awe, without laughter, drawing a long shuddering breath as she slipped into his arms.

His eyes were bluer than any sky, closing over her like the sky, darkening with desire. She closed her eyes, and there were lips on her lips, a questing mouth that drained her of strength in a languor of warmth and pleasure.

She felt the trail of his kisses on her throat, burning through the thin chiffon that covered her breasts, and the sparks ran through all the nerves of her body, faster and wilder like a spark on bracken in high summer, so that her whole body was filled with a breathtaking bright urgency.

And then she heard the words from a distance. They were soft, but they grew louder although they were only spoken once, and they began to echo in her head, as though they were being repeated over and over again. Leon asking, 'Do you know what you're doing?'

He spoke gently. Amused, maybe? She opened her eyes, and the fire went out, as suddenly as that.

No, she realised, but you do. You know exactly what you are doing. You are calling a halt and it should be me. I always call the halt, and that's how it was going to be tonight, except that tonight something went wrong with my defence mechanism. Something went wrong, and I think I went crazy.

She jerked herself upright and away from him, and her fingers twitched at the neckline of her dress. For no sensible reason, the neckline was where it had always been, but she moved instinctively as though trying to cover up every inch of herself.

'I rather thought you didn't,' he said.

Fran couldn't look at him. She had hardly touched the brandy in that glass, but that's what he thought it was, the wine and the brandy. She wished it had been. But it was him. She had lost her head because it was him.

She was clear-headed enough now. Nearly as cool as he was. She knew now what was happening, every inch of the way as Gerald had said.

Leon wanted her wanting him, but nothing that might mean an emotional entanglement because she was not that special. She was not special at all, and maybe Gerald was right again and Uncle Ted didn't yet know Leon's plans for the crafts shop.

Uncle Ted was an old-fashioned gentleman, who would expect Leon to act the gentleman where Fran was concerned. Uncle Ted would have been proud of him now—surprised at Fran but proud of Leon, who had so much self-control and was such a gentleman.

Now Leon was pouring Fran another cup of coffee, very black, because he was sure the brandy had gone to her head. Did he think she always acted like this after two sips of brandy?

She was cool. She felt as though there was a block of ice inside her where her heart used to be, and she hated him savagely, sitting there, pouring black coffee with a steady hand. 'All right?' he said, and he smiled as he gave her the cup.

'Fine. Just fine.' She hadn't realised it was scalding until she'd gulped some. It made her gasp and tears came to her eyes, and Leon took the cup away again, putting it down on the table.

'Take it easy,' he advised.

That was good advice. In future that was what she would certainly do. She never wanted to see him again.

She wanted to go home and she never wanted to see him again. She said, 'I think I would like to go home.'

He got to his feet the moment the words were spoken, as though he couldn't see her off fast enough, as if her pride hadn't had sufficient buffeting for one night, and she said silkily, 'I don't even like you. I'm only around because Uncle Ted has been so anxious that we should get on together.'

It was that or throw the coffee cup at him, and that hit. She saw him flinch and it made her feel a little better, although immediately he was expressionless, looking down at her with that cold mask of a face.

'You're a dutiful niece,' he said.

'Aren't I?'

'I'm sorry you've been put to so much trouble.'

'The meal was lovely,' she said inanely.

'Then that was some compensation.' He went to fetch her coat and she thought—I shouldn't have said that. It's almost true, but it was a stupid thing to say.

There was no taking it back, and she didn't really want to take it back, because it would stop Leon asking her out again. After that he would keep out of her way, and as far as she was concerned the Iceman was back in town. Her earliest impressions had been right. The warmth was only skin deep.

She held out her hand for her coat, she didn't want him putting it on her; and even when he opened the front door and it was still raining nothing was said. They reached the car and once inside that he turned on the radio, filling the silence with words that meant nothing.

But the silence was still there, and when the car drew up outside the Galleries, it seemed to Fran that it was nearly tangible. She was still angry, sick with herself, sick with Leon, and she couldn't think of anything that she would ever want to say to him again.

He walked round to the side door with her, and then she did say, 'Goodnight.'

'Are you all right?' he asked.

'But of course.' He watched her put her key in the lock and open the door. When she got inside she stood shaking, her hands clenched. She didn't move until she heard his car draw away, and then she went slowly and cautiously without turning on any lights, It wasn't late, but she didn't think she could face any talk about this evening's outing just yet.

It had not been a successful evening. The last half hour of it had been a horrible evening. She had made a 'proper Charlie' of herself and then acted like a spoilt child in a tantrum.

There were no lights on, Uncle Ted must have gone to bed, and that was a reprieve. Fran took off her shoes and crept along the passage, she was so anxious not to have him opening his bedroom door and calling down, 'That you, Fran? Did you enjoy yourself?'

She wasn't sure she could call back with any conviction, 'Yes, it's me. Yes, I did.'

She had offended Leon nearly as much as he had offended her, but she couldn't talk about it tonight.

For the first time since she'd arrived here Fran almost wished she could go back to Yorkshire. But she loved her work in the shop, and Uncle Ted did need her, and she could hardly run away because she had miscalculated Leon's feelings for her.

Gerald was right. With Leon every emotion was under tight control. He had no spontaneous feelings, like most human beings. She got out of her romantic dress and tried to smile. 'It's flameproof, non-combustible,' she had told Uncle Ted. That was Leon, and it was a pity it

121

wasn't her too. Ah well, she knew now that you can't set fire to an iceberg.

It was a long time since she had wanted to cry. Not since her father left them, and in a way Leon had caused those tears too, but why was she weeping now?

For herself. For a loving man she had dreamed up who wasn't there at all. Gerald's Leon was real. Fran's had been a dream and she was too practical to cry for dreams. But the tears still came.

She didn't sob nor make a sound, but even after she was in bed she could feel the tears trickling through her closed eyelids and like a tight strangling band around her throat...

She was up early. She hadn't slept well and when daylight came it seemed best to get downstairs and do something useful. She dusted the living room and prepared the vegetables for tonight's meal, and when Uncle Ted put in an appearance Fran was dressed and made up, on her second cup of tea and half way through the morning newspaper.

He was surprised. Neither of them usually had time to do more than scan the headlines before evening, but Fran looked as though she was doing some solid reading, and he asked, 'How long have you been down?'

'I woke early.' She had woken about two hours after she fell asleep, and for all her efforts with eyeshadow and mascara her eyes were less bright than usual. She smiled at him, his breakfast was ready. She poured his tea, and all the time he was watching her with growing concern.

'Everything all right?' he asked.

'Are you all right?' Leon had asked her last night ... 'But of course,' she said, as she had said then, and Uncle Ted said,

'I don't think so.'

He was bound to find out there had been a break between her and Leon. She drank a little of her own tea, to show how composed she was about the whole thing, and said brightly, 'I won't be seeing much of Leon from now on.'

'Why not?' Uncle Ted's early morning face, with the faint stubble of beard, looked grey and tired, as though these weeks of care hadn't helped him at all.

She said slowly, 'We had a disagreement last night. I don't think we particularly like each other. We just— went around together, and now it's over.'

'I see.' He sat down and she got up and went to the stove to fetch his breakfast. He seemed to be taking it for granted that Leon had made a rejected pass, because he said, 'You must choose your own friends, of course, and perhaps Leon is too much a man of the world for you.'

She nearly said, 'I'm not a child,' wondering if that was how both Uncle Ted and Leon saw her, as a 'crazy mixed-up kid'. But it wasn't funny, and if she was a child how was it that she felt a hundred years old this morning?

Compared to Leon perhaps she was immature, but Uncle Ted was an unworldly man, and in plain common sense Fran was a great deal more mature than he was. She had come here because she had sensed that he needed looking after, and now he was sitting there as though all his worries were winging back, weighing him down again.

She sat opposite him and said, 'Now you tell me what's wrong. What's going to happen now? You said Leon wasn't a man you wanted to offend, suppose I have offended him?' She made a grimace of a grin. 'By the way, he didn't take any man-of-the-world liberties last

123

night or anything like that, but I told him I didn't really like him, and I don't. There are times when truth will out, and last night happened to be one of them.'

She had to know how things stood and she went on, 'I've heard rumours that Leon has a personal interest in the crafts shop. Is that a fact? Could he really make things awkward for us?'

'He could bankrupt me tomorrow,' said Uncle Ted quietly.

That stopped her pretence of flippancy. For a moment she thought he might be joking, although it would have been a peculiar thing to joke about. She scanned his face, hoping against hope for some sign of teasing, a twinkle in the eye or an upturning of the mouth.

After what seemed a long time she asked huskily, 'How?'

'I owe him a great deal of money,' said Uncle Ted.

She should have looked at the accounts before, instead of staying entirely on the selling side, and playing at housewife and cook up here. Clerical work was what she was trained for, but she had enjoyed getting out of the office. She said, 'You ought to have told me.'

'I suppose I should have done.' He looked at his congealing breakfast as though he had lost his appetite. 'But it didn't seem necessary. Things have been improving, with Leon's help.'

'Just financial, is it?'

'He doesn't interfere, but——' Uncle Ted made an unhappy little gesture, and then a flicker of a faint smile touched his lips. 'He is all the shareholders we've got. He does have a say in how we're running the shop.'

She had been told by Gerald that Leon had had papers signed connected with the crafts shop, she had suspected he had a finger in the pie somewhere, but she hadn't realised that Uncle Ted was deeply in his debt.

He said now, 'I've always thought of this place as yours, and I thought once you'd met Leon, away from your mother and her prejudice, you'd be able to work with him.'

'Or for him?' muttered Fran.

Perhaps he didn't hear her. He said, 'Are you going home?'

'Am I what?'

'Do you want to leave here now that you know how things are?'

'How they are? You mean now I know we're in hock to Leon Aldridge?'

Uncle Ted looked like a guilty man, although she was sure he had always acted honourably, believing what he was doing to be for the best. It wasn't his fault the shop had come on hard times and she couldn't bear to see him so depressed.

'He won't bankrupt us,' she said with a cheerfulness she was far from feeling, 'while I've got breath in my body.'

'I'm sure he won't,' said Uncle Ted. His thin ascetic face was wistful. 'But I do wish you two could have liked each other.'

We might have done, thought Fran, if Leon had stayed the friendly business colleague instead of trying to be more than friend and less than lover. '*Please* eat your breakfast,' she begged.

He swallowed it to please her and she offered, 'I'll go round and make the peace if you like,' and as he looked up, hopeful and eager, 'I'll apologise for what I said. He thought it was the brandy anyway.'

Uncle Ted choked on a piece of bacon, and Fran patted his back with her first genuine smile of the day.

'It's all right, I was cold sober, and if I hadn't been I'd still have been safe as houses. Leon is a gentleman. He's a few other things I'm not over-partial to, but his worst enemy couldn't deny that.'

'Is it a bad thing to be?' Uncle Ted asked, and she gave him a hug.

'Of course not. It can be super, you're a super gent yourself. But I don't like him. Sorry, I am sorry. I'll work for him, though, if I have to, because this is our little shop and we're not going to let the shareholders down, even if he is the shareholders.'

Her reward for that was a smile from Uncle Ted, although she had no idea how she was going to word her apology nor if it would be accepted. It was bound to sound false. Leon would know her uncle had told her how things stood with the crafts shop, and that was why she was eating humble pie. And how was she going to say, 'I'm sorry I said I disliked you,' when she did dislike him?

'I'm sorry I said it,' she could say that all right, but he was no fool, that wasn't going to butter him up.

She was coward enough to think of phoning and apologising, she shrivelled inside at the prospect of confronting him face to face, but he might very easily answer the phone with others around. Although if she strolled into the Galleries and asked to see him that could be fairly public too. Unless she made an appointment.

She waited until his car was parked round the back, and then she went into the office and phoned the Galleries, and asked to speak to Leon. Whoever answered the phone—she didn't think it was Gerald—didn't ask her name. There was a constriction in her throat that made her voice squeaky, so that even if it had been Gerald he might not have recognised her.

126

'Leon Aldridge speaking,' said Leon.

'It's—er—it's Fran.' He said nothing, and she went on, 'May I see you? Could you spare me a few minutes?'

'Of course.' He didn't sound surprised nor interested.

'I'll be right round,' she said, and he put down the phone before she could.

He came to meet her as she walked into the Galleries, and took her through one of the doors that had no name on. It was all antique in here, desk, chairs, everything. Dark carved furniture that couldn't have changed since his great-grandfather's day. Or perhaps it was because she was feeling so gloomy herself that she found it oppressive.

He moved a chair a fraction for her, and she sat down meekly, while he stood with his back to the desk, as though he knew this wouldn't take long and he would soon be seeing her out again. He said, 'I presume you've been talking to your uncle, and he's told you why he's anxious that we should get on together.'

Colour flamed in her cheeks. She didn't have to say yes, of course he understood why she was here. She made herself look straight at him, although she hadn't much hope of reading anything in his face. 'He tells me you could bankrupt him,' she said.

'He knows that I won't.'

'Thank you.'

'Don't thank me. I'm not losing anything by backing Ted.'

'I'll bet you're not!' Fran hadn't meant to sound tart. That was her trouble, one of her troubles. Half the time she spoke as she was thinking, instead of slowing down and using a bit of discretion.

'I'm sorry,' she said. 'I'm sorry about last night too. I

127

shouldn't have said that. I do say things I shouldn't have said.'

'Forget it. Ted wants a business partnership between us, and I'm sure that will work out satisfactorily. We don't have to like each other for that.'

It was unlikely that Leon realised what a competent business woman she was, he had only seen her playing around, although the playing had been fun. She asked, 'Why *did* you take me around?'

He smiled and the charm was there, but his eyes were cold. They must always have been cold, even in desiring. She had imagined the warmth. 'Because you're decorative,' he said, 'and amusing.'

She sat with an even stiffer spine at that, jerking up her head, demanding, 'You don't like me either, do you?' and he said, quite gently,

'To tell the truth, girl, I've never even thought about it.'

She had blurted out the truth, that his cold-blooded nature repelled her although she admitted his surface charm. Now it was his turn to be brutally frank, telling her that when he wasn't with her she ceased to exist for him.

'I can believe that,' she said. 'Well, good morning.' As she walked towards the door he said,

'Don't worry Ted, he isn't in the best of health,' and that stopped her. She rounded on him, scared.

'He isn't really ill, is he?'

She felt that Leon would know, and when he said, 'He needs a break, he's worn down,' she was tremendously relieved that it was something she could do something about.

Why was Leon concerned? she wondered. Because he had money in the business, or because he *did* like Uncle

Ted? If it was affection perhaps there were some human feelings in him after all.

She said, 'If I could get him to take a holiday I could cope with the shop, I think. Would you give me any business advice I needed?'

'Of course. It would be in my interests.'

The phone rang on the dark carved desk and he turned, answering it with his back to her. She knew from his voice that he was speaking to a woman and that this wasn't a business call. He didn't say much, he rarely did, but he spoke of a date tonight, and she was certain it was Judith Waring on the other end.

It was as though she had become extra perceptive, and it was lucky she wasn't interested in him herself any more or this would have hurt.

He put down the phone with a word of goodbye, and said, 'Yes, I think you should persuade Ted to take a holiday. Except for those Christmas visits to you and your family he hasn't had a real break in years.'

'Mrs Mizon, who used to clean the flat for him, has a boarding house with her sister in Brighton.'

'Excellent.'

'You think I can manage, do you?'

'I've no doubt of it.'

He opened the door for her and she saw Gerald, and knew that he knew a call from Judith had been put through to Leon's office while Fran was in there. She was so nervily on edge that she seemed sensitive to all sorts of small signs. She could thought-read Gerald, who came over as Leon closed the door after her, and asked, 'Everything all right?'

Everybody seemed to be asking her that. 'Of course,' she said, and dropped her voice to whisper very softly, 'You're wrong, he isn't closing down the crafts shop.'

Gerald gulped and she relented. 'I didn't say you'd said anything.'

'Thanks,' he muttered.

'Thank you,' she said. 'That was the only thing you were wrong about.'

She gave him a brilliant smile, and went back next door to get things moving about Uncle Ted's holiday. Because it seemed to her then that her only hope lay in filling her life with as much action as she could cram into it, so that she would have no time for thinking about Leon and Judith.

That phone call *had* hurt. She couldn't imagine why. She didn't want Leon, she really did dislike him, but the thought of him with Judith made her ache.

It couldn't be her heart, because her heart wasn't involved. Her head ached, and her stomach ached. She was sick with an ailment she had never known before that was very like jealousy.

# CHAPTER SEVEN

UNCLE Ted put up all sorts of obstacles against taking that holiday right away. His main argument was that Fran couldn't manage yet. In another month or two maybe, but until then how could he leave her to deal with everything single-handed?

'I've always got Leon to run to,' she said drily. She wasn't likely to bother Leon unless she was in real difficulties, but in an emergency she could call on him.

'It's business as usual,' she'd told Uncle Ted, when she came back from the Galleries. 'And Leon says he thinks you ought to take a holiday. He says you haven't had one for years, and not to worry because he has every confidence that I can cope.'

She wanted Uncle Ted to have a rest, and she wanted to be very very busy for a while.

She started packing while he was still shaking his head, not sure what had hit him, but she was very persuasive and he finally agreed that he would go down to Brighton. A few days of sea air and rest would be a tonic, and Fran seemed sure she could manage. Besides, there was Leon next door.

She phoned Mrs Mizon and booked him into the boarding house for a couple of weeks, starting tomorrow. Mrs Mizon and her sister said that of course they could find room for Mr Reynolds any time, and it would be ever so nice to see him again.

That night Fran had a crash course on the office work. She went through accounts with Uncle Ted, through piles of correspondence. She wouldn't be doing any buying until he got back, but now she knew who provided what, and she also knew what kind of stake Leon had in this place.

That, as much as anything, made her determined to make the crafts shop a success. The potential was there. What was needed was drive and flair. She had the drive and she'd work on the flair, and some time they would pay Leon back, and that would be a real red letter day for Fran.

Uncle Ted, who had always thought she was the cleverest girl alive, wasn't surprised at the way she took in all these facts and figures. But she was concentrating so fiercely that she could hardly fail to assimilate them. She was glad to have something like this. It kept her mind off Leon and Judith, until she was alone in her room and too weary to hold back any more.

Leon and Judith were close. He would suit Judith and Judith would be an ideal wife for him. Fran believed it now and it couldn't matter to her, unless Judith persuaded him to close down the crafts shop, and that was unlikely.

Leon wouldn't mind getting emotionally involved with Judith, and with closed eyes and darkness all around Fran could see his house again. Judith's home was probably just as splendid, but Leon's Fran knew, and that was where she was seeing them now. Alone in that house.

She was shaken by the details that came into her mind, slow moving like a film being played, Leon making love to Judith, and by her own instinctive cowering reaction. She was hunched down, her arms over her head, as though she was out in the cold and shivering.

She sat up and shook herself, literally, because this was not on. This was lunacy. She was dead beat and she'd organised herself a hectic two weeks ahead, and she had to sleep, not lie here dreaming bad dreams, awake.

She shook up her pillow too, and told herself, 'Sleep, you idiot,' and not too long afterwards she did.

Next morning there was sunshine. Fran waved Uncle Ted off beneath a blue sky, reassuring him that everything was going to run like clockwork. But if it didn't she would either call in Leon, or ring Uncle Ted and Uncle Ted would come right back.

Considering how long he had run the shop without assistance, and profitably until recently, Fran, younger and stronger, felt it would be rather shaming if she had to admit that she couldn't. She wouldn't be calling in anyone if she could help it.

Sunshine got her off to a good start. The long-distance weather forecast said more rain, but weather forecasts were often wide of the mark, and today was just the day for a holiday or a fresh start. Fran went back into the crafts shop, and told herself she felt like a new woman.

She had a busy day. The sunshine brought customers, and she was even more delighted than usual to see them. She found time to make a phone call, accepting a standing invitation from the lady who made the samplers. She was going to get out as much as she could, because now that Uncle Ted was away there wasn't much to stay in the flat for.

One browser who didn't buy was Judith Waring. She came in during the afternoon, when Fran was handling two sales at the same time, and had another customer in front of a row of dolls—'characters from Shakespeare'—trying to make up her mind which to buy for her granddaughter.

Judith looked very stylish. Her fair hair gleamed beneath a black slouch hat. She wore white shoes, a white tailored trouser suit and a black silk shirt, and Fran was immediately conscious of the dust motes floating in the sunshine, and the bare boards of the unpolished floor, because Judith looked so immaculate.

Fran herself was warm and rather sticky. Her hair was anyhow, and she had been hauling merchandise about all day, so that her hands could have been cleaner. She hadn't looked at her face in the mirror since morning, so goodness knows what it was like.

She went on serving, giving Judith the smile she gave everyone who walked in, as soon as she caught their eye. Judith didn't smile—that could be something else she had in common with Leon. She raised smooth dark eyebrows a fraction instead.

When Fran got round to her she was still standing well back from the counters. 'Can I help you?' Fran offered.

'I shouldn't think so,' said Judith.

'Just—looking?'

'That's right.' Judith did what she had done at the theatre, eyed Fran slowly up and down, and Fran would have loved to say,

'This is my working uniform. I haven't changed radically since the last time you inspected me.' But that wouldn't do, with customers around, although it did seem that Judith was here just to look at her.

'I've a few minutes to kill,' said Judith. Before she went in next door to Leon, of course. 'And this is such an unusual little shop, isn't it?'

'Why, thank you,' said Fran. A crafts shop was hardly a rarity, and there was nothing outstandingly different about this one.

'Quite astonishing,' drawled Judith, and smiled then as though she had a good joke that she was keeping to herself. Whatever it was the laugh was on Fran, and she could only conclude it must have been something that Leon had told Judith about her.

She moved away quickly because a blush was burning from her head to her toes, and went to a customer the other side of the shop so that she could stand with her back to Judith.

When she turned round again, a minute or two later, Judith had gone.

Fran closed at the usual time, checked the till and secured the takings; and then went upstairs and took a soaking bath.

Half way through that, of course, the phone rang, downstairs in the office, and she answered swathed in a big towel. It was Uncle Ted. He had arrived safely, and everything seemed very comfortable, and he would have chatted for a while if he hadn't realised that Fran's teeth were chattering.

'Have you caught a chill?' he asked her, and she laughed.

'I could do any minute, I was in the bath.'

'Oh, my poor child, that wasn't very good timing, was it? Is everything all right?'

'Yes.'

'Goodbye then, I'll phone you tomorrow.'

'There's no need——' she began, but he had hung up, without giving her a chance to suggest that a rest meant a real break from business worries, not a day-to-day report on what was happening at the shop.

She was off for an evening with the sampler seamstress and her farmer husband. Before she went she fed herself on a tin of tomato soup and two rounds of toast, and she was washing the soup bowl when there was a knock on the communicating door.

Her fingers stiffened. She stiffened all over, and she had to make herself go and answer it. 'Oh, Gerald,' she said limply, and he must have thought she was at the end of her tether, because he stepped in as though prepared to catch her as she slithered to the floor.

But she stood quite upright and grinned. 'The sun was good for trade,' she said. 'I've earned my keep today.'

Perhaps he was surprised to see her smiling. He blinked a bit, and then he said, 'You're not—well, sitting around, are you?'

'What?'

'Sitting around. Thinking about things.'

It was nice of him to be concerned, but he had the wrong idea. 'I don't do much sitting around,' she said. 'I'm just going out, as a matter of fact.'

'Where?'

She hoped he wasn't going to start questioning her whereabouts again, but she told him, 'Visiting Mrs Aubrey and her family. She makes the samplers.'

That seemed to reassure him. 'She's a friend of yours, is she?' he asked, and Fran said,

'Yes,' although they had only talked when June Aubrey had come to the shop.

'What about Sunday?' said Gerald.

'All right.' She was going to accept all the invitations that came her way. She was going to fill every waking moment.

'What time? If we started early we could get down to the sea.'

'I'll need the morning to do the chores. About two o'clock?'

'It's a date.' He kissed her cheek, because as he went to

kiss her lips Fran turned her head.

'I'd rather you didn't use this door,' she said. 'It reminds me of that vase.'

It reminded her of Leon, and the sound of someone knocking on it jangled her nerves.

Gerald said that in future he would use the outer door, and if she needed anything and didn't want to come into the Galleries she could always phone him. He gave her his home number too, which was in the name of the folk upstairs so she couldn't find it in the book, and hoped she had a nice time tonight and hoped that the break would do Ted good.

'Thanks for everything,' said Fran, closing the connecting door and hearing Gerald snapping bolts on the other side.

Her mother would like Gerald. Fran liked Gerald. Fran had liked Arthur and a number of men before him. They were the safe ones and, as the old saying went, better safe than sorry.

She was sorry about Leon, and she was glad that she had June Aubrey to visit tonight, because Leon would be with Judith again and it was going to take a little time before Fran could think about that as calmly as she would like.

She had a pleasant evening, and arranged for the Aubreys to come and have supper with her next week. She came back lateish and slept soundly. She was coping well with the shop, and the weather stayed warm and sometimes sunny, until Sunday when they were back again with the rain.

It would have been nice to have had sunshine. Grey skies and drizzle were depressing, and Fran turned on the radio while she was cleaning floors and furnishings in the flat and the shop.

But the music didn't brighten her, and when the time came for Gerald's arrival she thought—I hope he's in a cheerful mood, I could do with a laugh.

She wasn't getting one. When she opened the door it would have been hard to imagine a more complete picture of misery. Gerald peered through bleary eyes behind his glasses, his nose was pink and his moustache drooped. He said, with an adenoidal accent, 'I've got a shocker of a cold. I feel awful.'

'You look awful,' she agreed, and added with quick sympathy, 'You shouldn't have come out in this. You ought to have gone to bed with a hot drink.'

He said lugubriously, as she drew him in, out of the drizzle, 'Who's going to bring me a hot drink? I thought I'd be better round here with you for an hour or two. I could do with some cheerful company.'

She choked back a hollow laugh at that. If he had looked one degree less seedy, or she had been one degree harder-hearted, she would have said, 'Sorry, but I need amusing myself, and I don't need your germs around the place, so you'd better go home again.' But she couldn't do that.

'Come upstairs,' she said, resigning herself. 'I'll stir up the fire and get you a drink and some aspirins. When did this start?'

Yesterday, he told her, with a prickling burning sensation behind the eyes and nose. He described his symptoms vividly, almost lovingly, and Fran began to suspect that Gerald was inclined to hypochondria. He seemed healthy enough, but he was making the most of a cold in the head.

She sat him on the sofa and made him a hot lemon toddy, and it was a grim day outside, so they were probably better off where they were. They watched television, read the papers, and Fran felt quite relaxed with Gerald, who was as comfortable as a pair of old shoes.

'What are you thinking about?' he asked her. He had looked up from the *Times* colour supplement and caught her watching him. She smiled.

'Oh, that we'd have been worse off if we'd gone to the sea for the day.' She couldn't tell him he was almost like having Uncle Ted here, and she asked, 'Isn't there really anyone who would boil a kettle for you where you live?'

'They would, I suppose,' Gerald admitted. 'They're all right. But living alone isn't home life, is it?'

'No.' Gerald had relatives all around; his parents were in Australia, to which an elder brother had emigrated. He wants looking after, Fran realised. He wants fussing and caring for. So many people did. Like her mother, like Uncle Ted.

She felt a little tenderness for him, because she was a kind girl. She could almost have gone over to where he was sitting on the sofa and hugged him and said, 'Cheer up, you'll find someone who wants to marry you and look after you one of these days.' But she didn't want to catch his cold, and if she had hugged him he would certainly have got the wrong idea. Fran was not applying for the post.

So she gave him some soup and sympathy, and tried hard to cheer him up, feeling like a sickbed visitor.

During the evening Uncle Ted rang for his daily report, although she had told him yesterday that she would be out today. 'It's raining again,' she said, 'so Gerald and I are watching television.'

He wasn't very interested in Gerald, but he was glad that Fran had company. While she was down in the office she rang the farm, and talked to Jim for a minute or two. She hadn't talked to him since she left, her mother loved answering the phone and always got there first if she could. Fran had always sent her love to Jim, and now she assured him that she was enjoying life and work in the crafts shop.

'I persuaded Uncle Ted to take a holiday,' she said. 'He's badly needing one, so I'm in charge, but it's all right so far.'

Her mother took over, as soon as she reached the phone and was told it was Fran calling, and Fran explained about Ted's holiday again. But her mother's reaction was quite different from Jim's. He'd thought Fran ought to manage, he saw no reason why she shouldn't be left in charge, but her mother screeched, 'You're not all on your own?'

'Yes. But I'm coping. The customers are all very nice, and as long as I'm nippy I can deal with them.'

'You're alone, though? All by yourself in the flat as well?'

'Yes.'

'I don't like it,' her mother announced.

'I don't think anyone's likely to break in here,' said Fran.

'I don't think Ted should have left you. You've only been there a week or two.'

'Five weeks.' It seemed much longer. 'And if I get any business problems I can always go next door for advice.'

'*Next door?*' Isabel shrilled, as though the highly reputable Aldridge Galleries were a house of ill repute, and Fran said to pacify her,

'Gerald works there, you know.'

'Ah yes.' Isabel didn't mind Fran going to Gerald for advice. It was Leon she couldn't endure.

'Gerald's here now,' said Fran. 'We were going out,

but it's horrible weather. How's the weather at home?'

Talk about the weather should be safe, but after a brief, 'It's raining,' Isabel returned to the matter that interested her and demanded grimly, 'Where's Ted staying? How can I get in touch with him?'

'I don't want you phoning up and bullying him. He needs this holiday.'

'I'm not having you put on,' said her mother, and Fran burst out laughing.

'As if Uncle Ted would put on me, or on anyone else, and you know I'm as strong as a horse.' As her mother started to protest she raised her voice. 'Now you take care of yourself, and Jim, and don't you worry about me. 'Bye now, and I'll ring again soon.'

'Anyone I know?' Gerald asked as she came back into the living room.

'Uncle Ted.' She sat down on the little hassock in front of the fire. The rain was pattering on the windows and she looked into the fire. 'Then I phoned the farm,' she said. 'I probably shouldn't have told my mother I'm trying to run this place alone. She's a worrier. And then, like a fool, I said I could always go next door for advice on the business.'

'What's wrong with that?' Gerald inquired.

'Leon,' said Fran, staring into a small glowing cavern. 'He's still her black beast. She's always blamed him for my father's going away. And for everything else.'

For his death too. In some things the past could always catch up with the present. It was in this room that Uncle Ted had broken the news to Fran, and her mother, that Peter Reynolds was dead.

'I had to say I'd be going next door to get your advice,' she said. 'If I'd mentioned Leon's name she'd have been down here like a flash.'

'You blamed him too, didn't you?' said Gerald quietly.

'Not the way she does.' She rested her chin on her laced fingers, elbows on her knees. 'I think he had to go, he had to get away, but he said that Leon had told him that an artist must be ruthless. I'm sure Leon did, I suppose it's true, but I always felt that was why he never even wrote a letter to us.'

Fran had waited, while Isabel became increasingly bitter and resentful. Any mention of Fran's father in those days had brought an hysterical outpouring of her mother's grievances. The money came, but no message and no address.

'You never heard from him at all?' asked Gerald.

'He sent money, but he never got in touch. Not even with Uncle Ted. I was sure I'd hear from him on my birthday, even if it was just a card.'

She smiled, remembering, her face turned away so that she didn't see Gerald's shocked expression of dawning realisation. 'He used to paint my birthday cards,' she said. 'Scenes, that's what he painted, with a little figure that was me—skinny with red hair. I often wish I'd kept them, but I was a child, and I thought they'd be coming for ever.' She sighed softly. 'But I would have liked one last card. It would have meant that he'd thought about me.'

'Fran.' Gerald came and put his arms around her, but she didn't want pity. She didn't know why she was talking like this, except that it was a miserable day, and Leon's name had come up somehow, and she had rambled miserably on.

She said, 'It was a long time ago, and you're here because you need cheering up, and here am I telling you my ancient troubles. Forget it, will you? Honestly, I thought I had. It's a bit of a laugh really, my mother still carrying a hatchet for Leon who's probably forgotten she ever existed.'

'So long as you're not still carrying a torch,' said Gerald sombrely, and she could look him straight in the face and laugh at that suggestion.

'Not me. I'm no torch carrier. Judith is very welcome to him.'

Gerald stared hard, then his face relaxed and he smiled too. He believed her. But of course he believed her, she was telling the truth, wasn't she?

Fran kept busy, and nothing happened that she couldn't handle for the rest of Uncle Ted's holiday. She saw quite a lot of Gerald, whose head cold passed through the usual stages. She went out most evenings, unless she invited guests to the flat. Perhaps she was doing a little too much, because when she stripped off her make-up last thing at night she looked pale, even drawn, in her bedroom mirror.

She was looking forward to having Uncle Ted home again. She needed someone around the place to talk to. First thing in the morning and last thing at night were dreary times when you were living alone.

She hadn't set eyes on Leon. She knew he wasn't there all the time, but he had been in the Galleries, Gerald had said so. She hadn't expected him to come round. He'd told her she could call on him if she needed any advice, but he wasn't likely to drop in uninvited until Uncle Ted came back. Nor invited, if the invitation came from Fran. They might be business colleagues, but they were no longer seeking each other's company.

Fran was sure Uncle Ted would be pleased with the sales figures. She had kept scrupulous accounts, dealt with the mail—by consulting him in her evening phone calls—and experimented here and there with displays.

She had worked like a Trojan, and she felt rather pleased with herself.

It seemed a pity that Leon wouldn't know. Uncle Ted might tell him, but Fran would have liked to show him the books, which were all her own work for this fort-night.

Leon had thought she could manage, he'd said so, but she had done really well and it would have been satisfying to hear him admit it. Because apart from being decorative and amusing, and having enough sense to run a smallish shop for a limited time, he didn't think much of her.

Gerald came round at midday on Wednesday. Uncle Ted had insisted that Fran should shut for a lunch hour, although she spent her time dashing around straightening shelves, eating a sandwich or a biscuit and drinking a cup of tea. Gerald had tried, without success, to get her out to lunch, he ate at a nearby pub with a bunch of cronies. But he often rang the side door bell at midday and asked, 'Coming?'

'Not today,' she always answered.

Today she asked, 'Is Leon in?'

'Yes.'

'Would you ask if he'd come round, if he can spare the time? I want him to see the accounts before Uncle Ted gets back tomorrow,' and as Gerald hesitated, 'He's got a share in this business.' Gerald didn't know how big the share was, but Fran had told him that was the situation. 'And Uncle Ted wants him informed how things are going on.' Which was near enough to what Uncle Ted had said.

'Yes, sure,' said Gerald, 'or you could catch him your-self. He's having lunch with Judith at——'

'I don't care what he's doing with Judith,' Fran snap-

144

ped, 'I can't march in on his lunch dates. All I want to do is give him an account of my fortnight's stewardship here, but I'll ring through to him this afternoon if you're too high and mighty to carry a message.'

'All right, I'll tell him,' said Gerald, looking hurt as she was about to shut the door in his face, and she was ashamed of herself.

'Sorry,' she said contritely, 'I didn't mean to snap.' She gave him what she hoped was an appeasing smile through the gap of the nearly shut door. 'I'll be glad to get Uncle Ted back,' she admitted. 'I think it is too much for me on my own. My health's all right, but it doesn't seem to be doing my temper any good.'

She took it for granted that Gerald *would* tell Leon, if he saw him that afternoon, but she wasn't so sure that Leon would spare the time to come round. It didn't matter. It was simply a courtesy on her part, showing that she accepted and didn't resent his interest in the crafts shop.

Uncle Ted had inquired several times if she'd seen Leon. 'No,' she'd said. 'Everything's all right. I haven't had to bother him.' But when Uncle Ted came home tomorrow he would be pleased that she had asked Leon round, and that she had been ready and willing to discuss the business with him.

It wasn't because she wanted to see Leon in particular. Of course she would have done the same with anyone who was backing the shop.

He didn't come during the afternoon, and that was sense, because she couldn't have left the customers. She could have shown him the books, but she couldn't have stayed to explain anything. If he was coming it would be when the crafts shop had closed. The Galleries sometimes stayed open later, so it could be any time at all. If he had an evening date it would be no time at all, and Fran wouldn't lose any sleep over that. It was just an idea, a courtesy.

She always took a bath after work, but today she made do with a wash, applying her make-up quickly, and not even changing her working clothes of jeans and pink and blue striped T-shirt, and sandals.

She fried sausages for her evening meal. She wasn't going out this evening, and she caught herself looking at the clock, and was irritated because this would never do, she was *not* waiting.

She had a dozen things to do after she had eaten her tea, which was also her lunch and dinner, and would probably be her supper because she wasn't very hungry.

She ate the sausages, washed up, and then she did some more polishing downstairs, and decided at last that he wasn't coming. She wasn't disappointed, it *didn't* matter. She had the office books and some of the correspondence and accounts on the living room table, and she might as well fetch them down into the office again, and then she would wash her hair.

That would prove to herself that she didn't give a hoot if Leon turned up or not. No girl gets her hair dripping wet if she's caring what she looks like.

But before she put the books away, or washed her hair, she stood on a chair at the kitchen window, because that way she could peer down on the spot where Leon parked his car. It was still there, which meant that he was too, and she realised that she was smiling. Not long after that there was a knock on the connecting door.

She didn't put on the light in the passage, she didn't want him seeing her too clearly in case she did something ridiculous, like blushing. There was enough light from the living room to see your way along, and she left that door wide open.

First sight of him caught her breath. 'Hello,' she said cheerfully. 'You got my message?'

'You wanted me to look over the accounts?'

'Yes.' She went ahead of him towards the living room, and in there the central light and a standard lamp were burning, as well as the fire. But she was all right now, and breathing normally. 'I thought they might reassure you.'

'Reassure me on what?' He looked down at the table and up at her.

'Your investment in the crafts shop,' she said. 'I've had two good weeks.'

'I'm glad to hear it.' He sounded polite rather than delighted, and she asked,

'Aren't you surprised?'

He wasn't surprised. 'Seasonal trade should be improving,' he said, which meant that if the customers weren't coming in increasing numbers now they never would be.

'I suppose so,' she had to agree. 'We even had sunshine, didn't we, the week before last?' She was getting no praise from him. 'Anyhow,' she said, 'I coped.'

'Of course you did.'

'And you don't want to see the accounts?'

'Not unless you're having problems with them.'

'No problems.'

But it hadn't been *that* easy. It had been no picnic. Fran had moved around a lot faster on her own two feet these last two weeks than he had. Leon never finished a day's work with his shirt sticking to him, as she had.

'Ted's back tomorrow, isn't he?' he asked suddenly. She nodded. 'Good,' he said, 'you're looking tired,' and she had to laugh at that.

'That's what I like to hear! I thought I'd done a really smart job. You can smell the lavender polish if you go down into the shop. I tell you, there's even a shine on the old floorboards. And every customer got served, and nobody asked to see the manager, and now you tell me sales should have gone up anyway because it's that time of year, and that I look as if I could do with a coat of polish myself.'

He was smiling as she was talking. When she drew breath he said, 'I'm sure you've done an excellent job, but I knew you would.'

'Oh!' Well, perhaps that *was* praise of a sort, and she went on quickly, 'If you don't mind, now that you're here, I would be grateful if you'd look through some of the paper work. So that I can tell Uncle Ted tomorrow that everything's checked and passed.'

She had no clue to what he was thinking. He didn't move for a few seconds, and he might have been wondering how he could word an excuse, although being Leon he was more likely to simply say, 'No.' Then he sat down.

'Could you get me a cup of tea?' he asked.

'Of course.' She brewed up and brought it, putting it beside him, then she sat down herself. Leon drank tea and went through papers, but he didn't query anything. The checking was brisk. This wasn't going to take him long, and she didn't want him hurrying away.

She liked him being here. He wasn't background company, like Uncle Ted and Gerald, but much more satisfying, as though having Leon in the same room was food and drink. She watched the bowed fair head, the strong hands turning over papers, and she felt stronger and healthier and happier.

148

Judith was there all right, there was no ignoring Judith, and Leon was only here because Fran had sent that message, but maybe there had been misunderstandings. She had said she didn't like him, and perhaps she didn't, but when he was near she felt complete. And that was odd, because she had never realised before that she might be incomplete.

When he finishes, she thought, I'll get some supper. I'll say I haven't eaten, and hope the fried sausage smell isn't still hanging around. I'll say I hate eating anything on my own—and she did, although until this last fortnight she hadn't realised that either; and I'll ask him what he's been doing lately.

Nothing to do with Judith, of course. Nothing about his social life, just work. He was in America earlier this week. She could always ask, 'What did you buy or sell in America?'

But until he finished going through the papers she sat very still and quiet, getting stronger every minute. She could feel security washing over her and her heart beat with delight.

When Leon closed the accounts book and looked across at her he said, 'Ted will be proud of you.'

'You said that before.' Joking, the first night he took her out, when she gave the girl at the Plover a trade card. The girl had come into the shop a day or two ago and bought a skirt very like the one she had admired on Fran. If Leon had remembered Fran could have told him that, but he said,

'Ted is always proud of you.'

'I'm proud of him. I'm lucky to have him.'

'Yes indeed.' He put a hand in front of his eyes for a moment, and taking it away blinked as though his eyes were troubling him. They looked heavy, and there was a fine-drawn tautness about the skin of his face. Now that Fran looked full at him she could see that he wasn't himself.

'You haven't caught Gerald's cold, have you?' she asked anxiously, and he smiled.

'I should have thought you were more likely to have caught that.'

She gave a small shrug. 'Not particularly.' She had been out with Gerald, but there had been no kisses to mention. Her proximity hadn't been much closer than the customers and colleagues next door.

Leon said, 'I've had an exhausting couple of weeks.' He grinned. 'Delayed jet lag.'

'Sounds nasty.' She hadn't thought that Leon could ever be tired, with his whipcord physique, but the responsibility for everything that happened in the Galleries was his. He shared it with no one, and he jetted between countries as other men took their cars from town to town. Her account books and pile of correspondence could have been the last straw tonight, after he had finished several hours of overtime in his own office.

She said, 'Sorry I bothered you with this.'

'That's all right.' As he stood up she jumped to her feet.

'Don't dash off. You do look bleary-eyed. Please sit down and I'll get some supper.'

'Don't bother about supper,' he said. 'But I've nothing to dash off for.'

No Judith tonight? But if Judith had been waiting he wouldn't have come. He sat in the chair Fran had seen him sitting in before, but this time Uncle Ted wasn't in the other armchair, and Fran took the hassock again, by the fireside. She said, 'I thought I was the one who'd had the wearing fortnight.'

'It seems we both have.' That could have a deep meaning, or only a literal one. She said lightly,

'I feel healthier than you look.'

'You look healthier than I feel.'

'There are some weird old bugs going around these days.' Her eyes danced as he quoted what she had said earlier.

'That's what I like to hear,' and she continued,

'But you look like plain old-fashioned 'flu to me.'

'Do I?'

'I'll get you my stepfather's cure.' She got up and he said,

'For 'flu?'

'For anything. You name it and Jim will mix you up a toddy.'

That was stretching the truth, but a hot nightcap was a universal remedy for chills and stress. Leon had been away until yesterday, so it wasn't likely he knew that she was making a habit of dispensing Uncle Ted's whisky medicinally.

She got the bottle out of the sideboard and poured some into a tumbler. Leon took it from her, and poured half the measure back into the bottle, saying, 'Steady on, I'm driving.'

Gerald had walked here on Sunday and Fran had driven him home. It had been raining then and it was raining now, but Leon had his car and he didn't like anyone else at the controls. He had promised her she could drive his car and she never had, and maybe she would remind him of that promise some time.

In the kitchen she boiled water, squeezed a lemon and added sugar, then carried the steaming glass back again to Leon, who asked, 'Am I drinking alone?'

'I don't have 'flu.'

'I very much doubt if I have.'

'All right.' Fran was anxious to keep this rediscovered camaraderie going. 'I'll join you, as a preventive measure.'

She made herself a weaker drink, and sat down again, and asked, 'What happened in America?'

'What happened here?'

'Nothing surprising. Just a seasonal rise in trade.'

Leon did look very tired, and she talked softly, about the shop and the people who had come in. Not Judith, she didn't mention Judith. She talked quietly, making him smile, taking him with her where she had been since she saw him last and Uncle Ted went on holiday.

She asked no questions, and neither did he. He never mentioned Judith either, nor Gerald come to that. He said very little and there were silences when you could hear the ticking clock, and the rain and the keening wind, and the soft rustle of coals settling on the fire.

She made up the fire once, poked it a couple of times, sending sparks up the chimney. It was very peaceful and it was getting very late. Fran wouldn't have moved. She would have sat here till morning, keeping the fire going, letting him rest.

He was resting, and so was she. They had both had two hard weeks and this was resting time. But he looked at his watch and said, 'I must go.'

She hadn't looked at the clock on the mantelpiece, and she didn't want to. She scowled at it now, as though it was an intruder. Leon would drive back to the island, and walk over the bridge and through the little wood, and across the lawns; and he would be wet through before he could get inside the house. And if that was the time it wouldn't be long before he would have to come back again to the Galleries.

She said, as anyone with any consideration would surely say, as late as this on a night like this, 'It's horrible outside. Why don't you use Uncle Ted's room? I could fix it in five minutes.'

There were no sheets on the bed, but the clean sheets were up there, waiting to be put on.

He said, 'Don't go to any trouble, but I'll take the sofa if that's all right.'

'Of course it is. Why shouldn't it be?' It was an old-fashioned horsehair sofa, long enough for him to stretch out. 'It isn't exactly the softest bed in the world,' she said, 'but if you put your feet up and close your eyes I'll get you a pillow and a rug.'

She brought them and he thanked her, and they said goodnight and she went to her own room.

She was tired. She didn't usually set the alarm, because she usually woke at the time she needed to wake, but she set it now. They had talked far into the night, and now she was alone she could hardly keep her eyes open long enough to undress and fall into bed. She felt that she might well sleep until midday unless something roused her, and better the alarm bell than Leon.

Not that she would mind Leon waking her, she thought drowsily, but she would look an absolute freak. She had tried to take off her make-up, but there could well be streaks of it left, and her hair would be like a bird's nest.

He would be asleep now, she was sure of it, he was more exhausted than she was. She saw his face, the tight-drawn skin over the strong bones, eyes closed; and it was as though she felt him breathing deep and slow beside her, and she could slip an arm around him and whisper, 'Sleep well. I shall sleep well. Outside it's raining and cold, but it's warm in here, and we are together.'

# CHAPTER EIGHT

THE alarm clock woke Fran. If it hadn't rung she would have slept on. As it was she had to resist the temptation to pull the pillow round her ears. She reached out, groping, to turn off the bell, then yawned and stretched and crawled out of bed.

A first glimpse of her face in the mirror was hardly refreshing. She looked a sight, and as soon as she was into her dressing gown she slumped on the stool in front of the dressing table, and brushed her hair.

She thought that Leon would still be asleep. She was almost certain that he would still be stretched out on the sofa, and in five minutes or so she would take a cup of tea along.

She opened her door very quietly and peered out into the passage, and heard movements from either the living room or the kitchen. She hadn't wanted him awake. She had wanted to wake him. And she certainly didn't want him seeing her like this.

She dived into the bathroom and washed her face, splashing cold water in her eyes, coming up clearer-headed, with her eyes quite bright and her eyelashes damp and spiky.

Leon was in the kitchen, standing by the window with a cup in his hand. 'Hello,' he said. 'I was debating about bringing you one.'

It was coffee. The jar was on the table. He looked as different as could be from last night, relaxed, refreshed, clear-eyed and calm; and suddenly Fran felt shy, unable to meet his eyes.

She went to the stove, lifting the kettle to check if

there was any hot water, spooning coffee essence into a cup for herself. 'There's a spare razor of Uncle Ted's in the bathroom if you want it,' she told him.

He fingered his chin, the fair stubble was less obvious than darker hair would have been, and said, 'I've got one next door.'

Do you often get ready for the day ahead next door? she wondered. Do you spend many unexpected nights away from home?

She stirred her coffee and said, 'Well, I'd better get dressed, it's nearly opening time.' She was backing out of the kitchen, but she caught herself at that and turned to make a more natural exit.

She couldn't get back into her room fast enough. She shut the door, and put down the cup from a shaking hand, and started to get dressed quickly. She was dressed, she was at the lipstick stage of her make-up, when she heard him walking along the passage, and then the closing door.

She was crazy, running off like that. She couldn't think why she had felt embarrassed. She had been perfectly properly dressed, covered by her dressing gown, but she had felt *shy*. That didn't happen often. She couldn't remember that happening since she was little more than a child.

She wouldn't have believed that she wouldn't have been able to drink a cup of coffee with Leon in the kitchen this morning, and talk naturally, without blushing or stammering or carrying on like a twelve-year-old.

She opened her door and grinned at the connecting door. 'Good morning,' she said brightly, 'I'm glad you're feeling better. I'm feeling better myself. I hope I'll see you again soon. Tonight perhaps when Uncle Ted is back? You will come round to see Uncle Ted, won't you?'

Of course he would come round to see Uncle Ted, and she was in high spirits, smiling to herself, as she finished her make-up and her cup of coffee, and went downstairs to open the shop.

The skies were grey again, but who cared? This was going to be a good day, and Uncle Ted was due home this afternoon. She would have a special meal ready for tonight. He'd said he'd been eating well but he was looking forward to coming home, and she'd slip out during the lunch hour and buy steaks, and make a fuss of his homecoming.

There were several customers in the shop when Gerald walked in. Fran had just finished serving, and was looking around to see which of the browsers needed attention, when she saw Gerald.

She smiled, but she got no smile back. He came to the counter and said, 'I want a word with you.'

'Make it quick.'

'Leon stayed here last night, didn't he?'

Gerald had probably been in the Galleries when Leon went back. Fran said, 'It was pouring with rain and he slept on the sofa.'

'It was pouring with rain on Sunday,' said Gerald grimly, 'but you got me home.'

They were talking quietly, but people were drifting around and even strangers were going to find this conversation enthralling.

'Excuse me,' said Fran, coming from behind the counter.

Gerald had followed her along and now confronted her, very close and talking very quietly. 'If I tell you something will you give me your word not to say I told you?'

She kept a happy face, and hoped she looked as

though it was happy talk, and nothing to interest anyone else. She said, 'I don't want any more confidential information. I don't want to be told anything else about Leon. You could write a book—maybe you should.'

There was a ballpoint pen on the counter. Gerald picked it up and took a scrap of paper out of his pocket. He wrote 'F.F.' with an ornate flourish and showed it to Fran. 'Does that mean anything to you?'

She went white. 'Why?'

'It's on a card in Leon's house.' She held the edge of the counter, because her legs were suddenly weak.

'I was going through a bureau drawer there about six months ago,' he said, 'we do business from the house as well as the Galleries, and I saw this card.'

Her eyes were very wide. She had never listened to him so intently before. She hung on his words now, as though she would drag them from him. 'It was a beach scene, rugged country, with a thin girl with red hair sitting on a rock. It was signed F.F. like that.' He glanced down at the initials on the scrap of paper beneath Fran's fingertips. 'Inside it said, "For my dearest girl. Happy thirteenth birthday." '

'I don't understand,' she said. But she did. She didn't need Gerald's explanation.

'Obviously he sent it to Leon to get to you and Leon didn't forward it.'

If it had come home her mother might well have torn it up and never shown it to Fran. Even Uncle Ted would have thought twice about handing over a birthday card, the way her mother was carrying on in those days. But Leon could have done it. He could have given her her last card from her father. Unless he had thought it might reunite Peter Reynolds with his family again, and that would be to the detriment of his art.

She asked huskily, 'Was there a letter with it?'

'I don't remember. I wouldn't have read it anyway. The card caught my eye and I picked it up.' She could understand how that could happen. 'I didn't know who F.F. was. They weren't your father's initials.'

'They were.' She smiled faintly. 'Fran's father. He always signed my birthday cards like that.' It was genuine. 'It's mine.' The colour was coming back in her cheeks, high and angry. 'And I want it.'

'You promised not to say I told you about it.' Gerald's voice dropped even lower. He looked over his shoulder, as though Leon might have followed him into the shop.

'I didn't.'

'*Please*, Fran,' he begged desperately.

There was still nobody really near. The customers were all chatting among themselves, and traffic noises drifted in from outside. A car hooter sounded angrily and Fran could have screamed with it.

This time she did smile, stretching her lips until the little muscles in her cheeks hurt. 'You stick your neck out, don't you? Then you jerk back under cover. You'll dislocate something, the way you're going on.'

Gerald looked wounded. 'I'm fond of you, that's why I'm here. But I don't want to lose my job and I don't want Leon turning against me.'

She stayed behind her smile. She took her hands off the counter and the tiny piece of paper fluttered to the ground. 'I can see that might be very nasty,' she said. 'All right, I won't say anything. But next time you're in the house you might pinch the card for me. He's not going to miss it and it is mine.'

'Oh, I wouldn't like to do that,' said Gerald hastily, and she laughed and patted his arm.

'You're the daredevil all right. I've got a knight in shining armour in you!'

She went across to the customers in the pottery section and told them what the good luck charms meant on the lucky mugs, and wondered where her own luck had gone.

Damn Leon, damn him for ever and ever. Having kept the card—why had he kept it?—but having kept it he could have given it to her since she came down here. Although then he would have had to admit, 'I not only advised Peter Reynolds to cut and run, I saw to it that, so far as it was in my power, he broke completely with his family. I held back the loving message that his daughter would have cherished all her life.'

She smiled and served and chattered, and she knew that this was the final blow. She daren't let herself think of Leon at all, or anger would have suffocated her. It seethed inside her, held down but burning.

She was almost scared to shut the shop at lunch time, because with nobody watching she could run amok and smash something.

All the time Leon had known that her father had thought of her. Just a week or two before he died that card had come for Fran. Of course there was a letter, if only to Leon, and Leon had known the address.

It wasn't out of the bounds of possibility that Fran could have got in touch and her father might have come to see her, or she might have gone to see him. Something might have happened so that he wasn't in the sea on that beach on the day he died. If Fran had received that card everything might have been changed. At the very least she would not have wondered, during these last eight years, if her father had ever really loved her.

But Uncle Ted would be arriving this afternoon. She

was cooking tonight and she had to shop at midday. So she did close and hurried upstairs to fetch her purse and a basket.

As she stepped out of the crafts shop Judith came round the corner from the forecourt, wearing a skirt that swished. It was green and finely pleated, and she wore it with a navy blue jersey blazer. She came straight for Fran, who said, 'Sorry, we're shut. Unless you're going this way to the car park.'

'I came to see you,' said Judith.

'Well, I'm off to the butchers.'

'This won't take long.' Judith stood squarely in her way. 'Just stop pestering Leon.'

Fran leaned back against the wall and inquired pleasantly, 'Had a little chat with Gerald, have you?'

'I was with Leon yesterday when Gerald gave him that message from you.' Judith and Leon had had lunch together, and so far as Fran was concerned they could have gone down with food poisoning together and it would have been all right by her.

'You wanted to see him on a business matter,' said Judith, with a curling lip and a scornful voice. 'Ha!'

'And?' prompted Fran, after about three seconds.

'You don't fool me,' Judith proclaimed.

'So you haven't had a chat with Gerald? Or maybe he's learning discretion at last.' Fran swung her empty basket. 'Then let me fill you in. Leon may have come round last night to discuss business, but he didn't leave till morning.'

She walked past Judith, who had fallen back a step and was croaking, 'I don't believe you!'

'Ask him,' said Fran, striding out. 'If you can believe him.'

Judith didn't follow her, so Fran must have given her

something to think about. She hoped that Judith would create a blockbuster of a scene when she next saw Leon, but she probably wouldn't. There had been other girls in Leon's life, and almost certainly other men in Judith's, although she seemed to be making heavy weather of Fran, as though there was something about Fran that particularly irritated her.

Anyhow, let them sort it out. She went round to the butchers and bought best grilling steak for two, although the way her luck was running today it could turn out as tough as leather.

When she came back from shopping she made the bed in Uncle Ted's room, and prepared the vegetables for tonight. She laid the table so that everything would be waiting and welcoming when he came.

After she opened the shop she stayed down there, and Uncle Ted arrived about half an hour before closing time. Fran had rarely been so glad to see anyone. She was serving when he came in, but she said, 'Excuse me,' and ran across and hugged him.

'It's good to see you,' she said. 'You look marvellous. Did you really have a good holiday?'

He looked fitter, he even had a slight tan, and she grinned, 'Where did you get that handsome tan? It's hardly stopped raining here.'

'Ah, but I've been out in the sea air,' he chuckled, enjoying her teasing and the warmth of her welcome. Until now his homecomings had always been to a closed shop and an empty flat. 'I had a very enjoyable time,' he said, 'but home's best,' and she gave him another hug.

'I've missed you,' she said. 'I must get back to my customer. I've been busy. I'll tell you all about everything tonight.'

He took up his case and came right down again. Fran

had coped well in his absence, but it was nice to know he had been missed.

She smiled at him over the head of her customer, and slipped upstairs herself shortly afterwards to turn on the vegetables. She no longer had all the responsibility, she could relax a little now, and the break had done Uncle Ted good.

As the last customer left, with the 'Do Come In' notice on the door turned to 'Sorry, We're Closed', she said again, 'Oh, I'm so *glad* you're back!'

'You haven't been working too hard?'

She shook her head emphatically. 'No, it's just good to have you around. I don't like being on my own. I did a bit of rearranging, have you noticed?'

'Very nice,' he said. Her displays were attractive and he approved of them all.

'And the window. Did you see the window?'

They went outside to look at the window. She hadn't put out the garden furniture during the last few drizzling days, so the forecourt was bare, but the window glowed scarlet.

She said, 'I stuck to one colour. Red this week. Anything with red in it is getting a look-in. I thought green next week. What do you think?'

'Very nice,' he said again, as Leon's car came through the archway. 'Hello there, my boy,' Uncle Ted waved vigorously. The car stopped and he went towards it. Fran froze, watching Leon get out and meet Uncle Ted and shake his hand with every appearance of affability.

'Good to have you back,' said Leon. 'You look better for it.'

'I am.' Uncle Ted turned to include Fran. 'Fran's managed very commendably, hasn't she?'

Judith had told him what Fran had told her. His face

was calm, but Fran knew he was angry. 'She's just showing me her window dressing,' said Uncle Ted, and Leon walked swiftly over, reaching her several paces ahead of Uncle Ted, and long enough to say quietly and savagely,

'What the hell is it with you, or are you just a natural troublemaker?'

She wanted to ask, 'Did you have trouble explaining to Judith?' but she couldn't, and that wasn't because Uncle Ted was with them by then. It was because if she opened her mouth she would spit at him, 'Why did you steal my birthday card?'

She kept her lips tight and thin, and Uncle Ted said, 'She deserves a holiday herself, doesn't she?'

'She deserves something,' said Leon blandly.

He talked for a minute or two longer with Uncle Ted, about Brighton, but Fran went inside out of the drizzle, and away from Leon.

She was bashing the steak—to make sure it was tender, and because she felt like bashing something—when Uncle Ted came into the kitchen.

'You didn't see much of Leon while I was away, then?' he said.

'He looked at the books. Did he tell you that?' He hadn't. 'Well, he did, last night, and he said trade usually improves around now but the figures are good.' She suggested, 'Would you like to have a look at the paper stuff while I finish this?'

She couldn't tell Uncle Ted about the birthday card. She had promised Gerald, and Uncle Ted was in Leon's debt so they had to stay on friendly terms.

She would get that card one day, though, if she had to burgle the house on the island herself. No, she wouldn't. Of course she couldn't get inside the house unless she was asked in. She'd never get a chance to turn over Leon's bureau drawers.

It shouldn't matter too much. Just knowing that her father had sent her a birthday card was what mattered. That should make her happy. It did make her happy. Her father had remembered her birthday and sketched her where he was, because that was where he wanted her to be. But she still felt deeply and bitterly betrayed.

She went to call Uncle Ted when the meal was ready; and the steak was tender, and afterwards they sat in the living room by the fire and she asked all about his holiday, and thanked him for the two picture postcards he had sent her which she had stuck up on the kitchen dresser.

He had also sent her mother and Jim a card, and Fran hoped her mother wasn't still indignant about Uncle Ted leaving her in charge. When she told him, she thought it was funny, he looked apprehensive.

'A good job you didn't give her your address,' Fran joked. 'She was for going down after you, or phoning you up.'

'Oh dear! You don't think she'll be coming here?'

'Wild horses wouldn't drag her,' said Fran. 'And you don't need to answer the phone, or if you do and it's Mother you can always say it's a wrong number.'

Uncle Ted hated upsets. He had suffered from Isabel's scenes in the old days before Jim took over. Fran was teasing him, because Jim would always stop Isabel making too much of a fuss.

'Jim said he was glad you were taking a break and he knew I could manage,' she said reassuringly. 'And I did, didn't I?'

She was sitting in a chair tonight, instead of on the hassock. That made it different from last night, when she

164

had been here telling Leon about the things that had filled the past fortnight for her.

She went over them all again now, for Uncle Ted, where she had been and what she had done, in greater detail than she had reported in her phone calls to him.

After he had listened for a while he said doubtfully, 'I think you overdid it, my dear.'

'Overdid what? The gay life?' She wrinkled her nose. 'I had a very mild time really.'

'Not many early nights, though. You look tired.'

'So they tell me.' So Leon had told her last night, and she was suddenly on the brink of tears, so that she had to duck her head and blink furiously, putting a hand in front of her eyes. Leon had done that too, he had been tired too.

'An early night tonight,' said Uncle Ted firmly.

Fran took a book to bed with her, and read until her eyes blurred and smarted, but even then it was hard to sleep.

If only the sun would shine! It was raining again next morning and Fran put on her brightest lipstick and wore a scarlet shirt with her jeans. But instead of livening her up that only seemed to exaggerate everything that was wan and wistful about her face today.

She worked hard at being cheerful, but more than once she caught Uncle Ted looking anxiously at her. With him back she was less busy in the shop, of course, and during the afternoon there was a slack period when they both waited for customers.

In the silence Fran gave an involuntary sigh and Uncle Ted asked at once, 'What's the matter?'

'Nothing.' But she *had* sighed. 'I just wish the sun

would shine. I've got a bit of a headache—it's these heavy black clouds.'

'Why don't you take a walk round the market?' he suggested. 'I can manage here. Have an hour or two off. Have the rest of the afternoon.'

That was a tempting offer. It was raining, but she fancied a walk. Down to the river, perhaps. 'Are you sure?' As she spoke he chuckled.

'Don't think you're the only shopkeeper in the family! I ran this place before you were born, and now I'm just back from two weeks in Brighton I'm as good as twenty years younger.'

'You mean I'm not indispensable?'

'Not for this afternoon.'

She wouldn't take the whole afternoon, just an hour or two, and she put on a mackintosh and tied a scarf round her hair. When she came downstairs the shop had several customers, and she grinned at Uncle Ted. 'If you're rushed off your feet,' she said, 'don't blame me.'

He was happy to see her laughing, but he didn't see the laughter fade as she stepped outside. Nor how she hurried past the Galleries with her face averted, looking at the pavement and the traffic. Leon wasn't likely to be standing around, staring out, but she wasn't risking it.

She walked fast, over Clopton Bridge, and along the towpath to the meadows and the weir. The river was high and wide, and the rain still came steadily down. But she felt that it was doing her good, washing away her headache if not her depression.

She watched the swans, riding the swell of the water, magnificently unperturbed, and passed a few determined characters who didn't care about the rain.

Then she went round the market, chatted with a girl with whom she had gone to school, and who was now married, with a lively three-year-old boy in tow; and bought a large bunch of yellow tulips. If she put them in a vase in the flat it would be the next best thing to sunshine.

She had been gone about two hours, which made the time not quite five o'clock, but when she returned the shop was shut.

She thought the Closed notice on the door was a mistake, that somehow it had got turned, but the latch didn't open the door, and when she peered through the old green glass panel she saw no movement, and no lights, and rang the bell, alarmed. Something was certainly wrong.

She kept her finger on the bell and her nose pressed to the glass panel, so that she saw Uncle Ted before he opened the door and thanked heaven for that.

'What's ha——' she began as the door opened, and he caught her arm and yanked her in.

'Your mother's here,' he hissed. His grey hair was standing on end, he must have run his fingers through it at least half a dozen times. He was wild-eyed with agitation and whatever her mother had done to upset him like this was inexcusable.

'It's never about you taking a holiday?' Fran gasped.

'No.'

'Is Jim all right?'

Uncle Ted gulped, but his voice still sounded strangled. 'She arrived in a taxi about ten minutes after you left, and she went straight in next door to see Leon.'

'What?' Fran felt as though someone had hit her over the head with something very large. 'Why?' she croaked.

'Someone phoned her this morning, and told her Leon was living here with you while I was away.'

The enormity of that rendered Fran speechless. Gerald must have gone out of his mind to do that. He knew how her mother would react, Fran had told him herself that if she'd so much as said that Leon was even giving her business advice her mother would have gone spare.

'Gerald?' she whispered incredulously.

'A woman,' said Uncle Ted hoarsely, 'who didn't give her name.'

There was only Judith. It was quite likely that Judith knew how pathological Fran's mother was about Leon Aldridge.

'It isn't true,' Fran groaned. 'But what a horrible *mess*!' She couldn't bear the thought of her mother facing Leon with that fandangle of nonsense. How could her mother do that? How could Jim let her? 'What did Leon do?' she asked.

Uncle Ted looked punch-drunk. 'She'll tell you,' he said, and he went slowly ahead of her up the stairs from the shop to the flat.

Her mother was in the living room, lying on the sofa, and the place reeked of eau-de-cologne. She must have emptied a bottleful. Usually she dabbed a handkerchief with it when she had a headache, but this was more than a headache. She had raised herself on an elbow, and she was waiting for Fran to come through the door.

The moment she did her mother wailed, 'Fran, how *could* you?'

'How could I what?' Fran dropped the bright yellow flowers on the table, and clenched her hands in frustration. This was her mother in the mood of unreason that was like beating your head on a brick wall. She hadn't been like this for years and years, but now they were right back to those early days.

'Leon came round here to check the accounts for me.'

Fran raised her voice. If she shouted some of it might get through. 'It was pouring with rain, he was dead beat, and he spent the night on that sofa.'

Isabel leapt from the sofa as though it was contaminated. 'I am not having an affair with Leon!' Fran was near the end of her own self-control. This had put her into the most humiliating situation of her whole life. 'Is that what you said next door?' How could she stay here now? How public had that scene been? What would Leon do about this?

'What did you do, for pity's sake?' she moaned. 'Rush in and start screaming, like the last time?'

'How could you?' Isabel demanded again, her voice quivering like a child's who finds the whole world against her.

How could Fran remind her of the last time, she meant, and she began to cry, tears rolling down her cheeks. She had the knack of easy tears, she could weep happily when a TV play piled on the pathos, and although Fran loved her she was in no mood now to comfort her.

She found herself laughing. 'Judith, me, and now you,' she said. 'Leon must have had his fill of hysterical women.' Her laughter was close to hysteria and she bit hard on her lip to stop it. 'What did he say?'

'He's evil.' Isabel might be weeping, but she wasn't relenting. She still blamed Leon Aldridge for everything. 'He said it was all my fault.'

'What was your fault?'

'Your father going away.'

'So it was.'

It was the first time Fran had ever said that. It was the first time anyone had said it except, apparently, Leon just now.

169

'Fran!' Her mother was stricken to the heart, and Fran went furiously on.

'And this anonymous phone call, you believed it? You didn't phone me? You didn't even come in here first and try to see me or Uncle Ted? I don't think I'll ever forgive you for that!'

'Because I knew something like this would happen when you came down here.' Her mother turned on Uncle Ted, who was practically wringing his hands in the background. 'I knew you'd meet that man and he'd take you away, like he took your father away. And he's evil. He's got no heart. The things he said——'

'Be quiet, you stupid woman!' Uncle Ted bellowed, with a vehemence Fran could never remember in that gentle man before. It left Isabel gasping. She stared at Ted, her mouth working but no sound coming out as he went roaring on, 'Leon has been like a son to me. I would have been delighted if he and Fran had fallen in love, and I wouldn't have cared if he had been staying here. I'd have been glad to hear it. He's an honourable man, a fine man. Fran couldn't have found a better man in the length and breadth of this land.'

'You're mad!' shrieked Isabel, high and shrill.

'Oh no, I'm not.' Uncle Ted's voice dropped to a growl. 'But you are, about Peter and Leon. It's because of you that Fran can't forgive Leon, although God knows there's nothing to forgive.'

'I won't listen!' Isabel clapped her hands to her ears, and rushed out of the room into the passage, and Uncle Ted shouted after her,

'You ought to thank him. He knows Peter wrote to you and you never answered and you never let Fran know.'

Isabel stopped dead, and slowly turned round. 'That is

a lie,' she said, her voice catching between each word, and Fran knew it was the truth.

'It's no lie,' said Uncle Ted. 'But Leon never told Fran. Did he?' He looked at Fran, and Fran shook her head jerkily; she couldn't speak. 'No,' said Uncle Ted. 'He said to me, "The girl's lost her father, we can't do anything that could turn her against her mother now." '

Isabel came very slowly back, with dragging steps, as though she was being pulled in against her will. 'Peter never sent any letters,' she whispered.

'Isabel.' Uncle Ted's anger had ebbed away. He wasn't shouting at her any more. 'I know. Peter phoned me and asked me to give you a letter, because you returned every letter he sent you, but I knew what would happen if I did. You'd have torn it to pieces and thrown it in my face. I wasn't on Peter's side at the time. I felt he'd left me with enough trouble, and I told him he'd better stick to the postal services.

'I've blamed myself since, but what difference would it have made? Except that Fran might have taken her father's side, and how would you have been then? It would have destroyed you.'

Isabel picked up a flower, and sat down on the sofa, looking at the yellow tulip as though she was talking to it, because she couldn't face the two pairs of accusing eyes.

'He deserted us,' she said in a little-girl voice. 'He left us, and just to *paint*. I could have understood if it had been another woman, but just because he wanted to paint pictures.

'What was the use of writing and saying how beautiful it was where he was, and how he could get a cheap house and we could go out to him? It was primitive out there. What did he think we were? Gipsies? And there was Fran's schooling and——'

Fran found her voice suddenly. 'He sent a card for my birthday. To Leon.'

'Yes,' said Uncle Ted.

'You knew?' She stared at this strange Uncle Ted, who knew so much. 'Why didn't Leon give it to me? Why didn't you tell me?'

'It went to your home first, didn't it, Isabel?' Isabel said nothing. 'And she returned it,' he told Fran. 'Then Peter sent it to Leon, and asked him to try to give it to you, but by the time it reached Leon Peter was dead.'

Isabel gave a convulsive sob, but Uncle Ted still looked at Fran. 'That's when Leon said "The girl's lost her father, we can't do anything that could turn her against her mother." '

She should thank Leon for that. To have been torn by divided loyalties at that time of tragedy would have been traumatic. 'He kept the card,' she said. 'Why hasn't he given it to me now?'

'I don't know. But I never told you because it would have been opening an old wound for Isabel,' said Ted grimly. 'Although why I should concern myself with her feelings when she never considers anyone else's I do not know.'

The tears were running down Isabel's cheeks, and Fran said, 'Oh, Mother, do stop crying. Why ever did Jim let you come?'

'He'd gone to a sale,' Isabel sniffed. 'I wasn't expecting him back until about now. I left him a note.'

Fran smiled weakly. 'What did you write? "Off to save Fran from a fate worse than death"? Although if I was supposed to have been living with Leon for a fortnight it might have been rather late to come charging to the rescue.'

'What are you laughing at?' Isabel glared through her tears.

'If I don't laugh I'm going to burst into tears,' said Fran, 'and I don't think Uncle Ted could stand the two of us howling. I'm going to try and phone Jim. You make a cup of tea, or put the flowers in water, or something. Don't sit there, dripping all over the tulips.'

She took off her headscarf and mac and put a hand on Uncle Ted's arm. 'I'm sorry we've made things so grim for you.'

He covered her fingers with his own, giving them a comforting little squeeze, and she went down into the office and dialled the farm's number.

She got Jim. She got out, 'It's Fran,' and he said,

'Hello, how are you? Your mother doesn't seem to be around.'

'There's a note.'

'A what? Oh!' He was obviously spotting it for the first time, by the telephone.

'What does it say?' she asked.

' "Had to go down to Ted's to see Fran. Will phone you," ' he read. 'What's up, then?'

'A lady who has a vested interest in Leon Aldridge phoned Mother and told her he was staying in the flat with me while Uncle Ted was away.'

'Was he?' Jim sounded interested.

'No. Unfortunately. But she arrived here by taxi and went storming into the Galleries to accuse him of seducing her only child.'

Even Jim's stolid nature was shaken. 'My God!' he gasped.

'That's right,' said Fran. 'We haven't heard what Leon

said on that point, but he did tell her she was to blame for Father leaving home. She came round here in such a state that Uncle Ted had to shut the shop, and now she's up in the living room getting her breath between hysterics.'

'Poor lass,' said Jim.

'Poor Uncle Ted,' she said. 'Leon's got a massive stake in this business, and I shouldn't think Mother's endeared him to the family. I suppose you don't have a lot of money you'd like to invest in case Leon asks for his lot back?'

She knew that Jim's capital was all tied up and that he was far from being a rich man. He couldn't help Uncle Ted no matter how much he wanted to.

'I'm sorry——' he began.

'I didn't mean it. I just can't stop chattering. It's all been so awful.'

'You're fond of Leon Aldridge, aren't you?' said Jim quietly.

'What makes you think so?'

'You did say—unfortunately.'

'What?' She couldn't follow that, but she said, 'Yes, I am. Very.'

'Tell your mother I want to talk to her.' Jim was his solid, steady, reliable self. 'And then I'll come down and fetch her. This nonsense has got to stop.'

'She doesn't deserve you,' said Fran.

'She suits me,' said Jim. He often said that, he meant it too. 'And I reckon if you had a word with Aldridge he'd understand. This isn't your fault.'

Jim didn't know the whole story, but she tried to be comforted.

Isabel came down to the phone with a mutinous expression, and returned looking like a martyr, suffering but saintly. 'I'm going to lie down,' she announced, and locked herself in Fran's room.

'Let's hope she stays there until Jim comes,' said Uncle Ted, who was putting the tulips in a jug. Fran thought she would.

She went down to the phone again herself, and rang the Galleries. The little time the bell was ringing she prayed, both for courage and that she would somehow find the right words to say.

Mr Aldridge wasn't at the Galleries, she was told, not by Gerald, perhaps she would care to try his home number.

She said, 'Thank you,' and wrote it down in funny shaky figures. If he wasn't there, or someone else answered, she couldn't take this any further just yet. She was feeling queasy with apprehension, and she groped her way into the chair behind the desk.

'Leon Aldridge speaking,' he said.

She said, 'This is Fran, I can't begin to apologise——' and he said crisply,

'Then don't. It wouldn't be a rewarding discussion.'

With which he hung up on her.

# CHAPTER NINE

FRAN went back upstairs to Uncle Ted. The jug of tulips was on the draining board, and he was sitting at the kitchen table waiting for the kettle to boil on the gas ring. He looked as though he needed a cup of tea, and she told him, 'I tried to phone Leon, but he doesn't want to talk.'

'Can you blame him?' he asked her.

'No.' In no way. She could do with a cup of tea too. Her throat was as parched as though she had been walking through a desert. 'It had to be Judith who phoned Mother,' she said. 'She knew Leon slept here Wednesday night.'

'It sounds as though she was jealous.' Uncle Ted got up to reach for the tea caddy, and Fran couldn't think of any other explanation herself.

'There's no reason, but I suppose she must have been.' Leon wouldn't be too pleased with Judith either. Judith was as much to blame as anybody for the scene next door, and tomorrow Fran would phone and apologise again.

But tomorrow might be too soon. Perhaps she should give him longer than that to calm down. A few days, even a week. Or she might write him a letter. He would surely read a letter.

They drank their tea, and then she sat down at the living room table, with a writing pad, and tried to explain. But an hour or so later she had written little.

Please let us be friends, her thoughts ran, because I want that so very much that I don't know what I shall do if you won't listen. You *must* listen. I'm frightened. I

176

don't know what to say, but I'm afraid that I'm in love with you, and what shall I do if you won't listen?

It was dark outside now. Her mother hadn't emerged, and was very likely sleeping like a baby. Uncle Ted had been reading the newspaper for a long time—or pretending to read, and Fran knew that she couldn't wait, not even till morning.

If she phoned again Leon could just hang up on her again, but if she went to his house he surely wouldn't refuse to see her. She picked up her mac from the chair on which she had dropped it, as Uncle Ted looked up. 'Do you mind being left with Mother?' she asked, and he gave her his lopsided smile.

'I shall barricade the door with furniture to stop her getting out until Jim arrives.' She smiled at his little joke. 'But where are you going?' He sounded apprehensive. 'Not to see Miss Waring?'

'Judith? Not likely. I'm going to try to see Leon.'

He wasn't much happier about that. 'And I don't know that that's advisable.'

'I don't suppose it is,' she agreed, and grinned. 'But if he loses his temper and really has a go at me he might feel he has something to apologise for when he calms down. That might even things a little.' She left the rest unsaid. Besides, she *had* to see Leon, and try to make the peace. She couldn't sleep on it.

'Don't expect him to listen to you,' Uncle Ted warned her.

'I don't.' Fran dropped a kiss on the top of his head and hurried off.

It was a wretched night. She kept the wipers going all the way, but they hardly cleared the streaming windscreen.

'Rain, rain, go away, come again another day,' the

childish jingle ran through her head. She was being childish. She was being as impulsive and as silly as her
mother, but she kept the car heading down river until
she turned off the road and drew up in front of the coach-
house.

As she got out a window opened above, and a woman
shouted down, 'Can I help you?'

'I want to see Mr Aldridge.'

The woman was probably the housekeeper, now cran-
ing her neck for a good look at Fran in the lights from
the flat. 'He's over at the house,' she said, 'but the river's
very high. You want to be careful crossing that bridge.
Have you got a torch?'

'Yes, thank you,' Fran called back, and the window
closed.

She got the torch out of the side pocket of the car. She
still hadn't replaced the batteries, so it was even fainter
now than it had been the night Leon used it to look at
the engine when Poppy broke down.

It glimmered in front of her on the path down to the
river, and the bridge, and when she reached that she
stopped. The river was high. The slats of the bridge were
under water so that only the handrails marked it. Walking across would be a risk, although if you held the
handrail you could still get over.

She hesitated briefly, then paddled into the water,
catching her breath at the chill, and at the surprising
deepness because very soon it was knee-high. It was
flowing fast, tugging, and she had one wild moment
when she put down her foot and a slat was missing. She
grabbed frantically for the handrail with both hands,
dropping her torch.

The torch hadn't been much use, and although clouds
hid stars and moon her eyes were used to the dark so

that she wasn't much worse off without it. But after that she moved very carefully. Her instinct was to get across the bridge fast, but she had to test for every step. She had no idea how many of the wooden strips had been swept away.

She reached the other side with very real relief, and squelched her way through the trees and across the lawns to the house.

Leon might feel like shutting the door in her face, but on a night like this he would have to let her in, and although she was apprehensive about facing him she was desperate to get under cover.

She rang the front door bell, and shivered for what seemed ages, getting no answer. There were lights on, the woman had told her he was here. He couldn't know who it was, so why didn't he answer?

Even under the porch the rain reached her. Not that that mattered, she couldn't get much wetter, and she *had* to get inside, she couldn't risk the bridge again. She put her finger back on the bell and held it there, and after another long minute Leon opened the door.

He was barefoot, in slacks and open-necked shirt and a dark green silk dressing gown. He looked as nearly dishevelled as she had ever seen him, hair ruffled, eyes heavy-lidded. She stuttered, 'Oh, sorry, were you in bed? I mean are you alone? I mean——'

He looked at her and she felt as though she had been pushed away. 'What the hell are you doing here?' he said wearily.

'I came to apologise. You wouldn't listen to me on the phone, would you?'

'Go home.'

'I don't think I can.'

'What?'

She lifted a foot. Her shoe was thick with mud and her jeans had a high tidemark well above the knee. 'It was this high when I came. One slat on the bridge has gone and I suppose the rest are being loosened.'

Leon moved aside and she walked in. She had only taken a couple of steps when she saw her footprints on the grass green carpet and stood still. He left her there, and came back almost at once wearing wellington boots and a trench mac, and carrying a heavy torch. 'Where are you going?' she asked unnecessarily.

'To look at the bridge.'

He'd find it as she'd told him. When she was alone she called 'Hello'. Nobody answered, but that didn't mean no one was here, although there was an empty feel to the house. It was warm but empty, a showplace.

She had marred some of its perfection with her muddy shoes, and before she dared take another step she took them off. Then she made her way to the kitchen, carrying her shoes, and got out of her mac and rubbed her feet and her hands to warm herself up.

When she heard Leon call, 'Where are you?' she went quickly to the kitchen door.

'In the kitchen.'

There was plenty of mud on his boots too, he must have left an awful mess on the carpet, and why she should be thinking about that she didn't know.

'You're crazy,' he said. 'Did Ted know you were coming here?'

'Yes.' Yes to both. She agreed that she must be crazy.

'You'd better ring him. I presume your mother doesn't know?'

She smiled with unsteady lips. 'She's been in my bedroom for ages. Jim's coming down to fetch her. When I left Uncle Ted said he was going to barricade the door to stop her getting out.'

There was no answering smile to that weak joke, and she padded barefoot after him to a telephone on a small gold and white ormolu table in the hall.

He stood listening while she told Uncle Ted, 'I'm at Leon's, and the river's over the bridge so I probably won't be able to get back till daylight. Is everything all right?'

'If you mean is your mother still sulking,' said Uncle Ted grimly, 'the answer is probably yes. I can hear her moving around, but I'm expecting Jim any time now, so even if she does emerge I think I shall survive.'

'Of course you will,' said Fran, and Leon held out a hand for the receiver.

'Ted?' he said. 'Why did you let her come here?' Fran could imagine Uncle Ted's indignant, 'How could I stop her?' and Leon said, 'No, I suppose you couldn't. Well, I'll get her back as soon as I can.'

As he put down the phone she said, 'I'm not a package for delivery, you know. I'll get myself back.'

He sighed, as though she was a wearisome problem. 'Why don't you try it now? We might both get lucky.'

'All right.' But she knew he couldn't let her and he said,

'There's a fire in the drawing room.'

He turned, he wasn't going in the direction of the drawing room, and she said, 'Won't you even listen to me? It wasn't my fault my mother said whatever she said. Somebody phoned and told her——'.

'She told me what they told her,' he said curtly. 'Are you sure it wasn't you?'

She gasped, 'Why would I——' and again he didn't let her finish.

'I don't know,' he said heavily. 'I simply don't know. Why did you tell Judith I stayed the night?'

'Because she told me to stop pestering you and that shut her up.'

'You'd better get dry,' he said abruptly, and Fran looked down at her wet and muddy jeans.

'I'm not dressed for the drawing room.'

'You're going to catch your death in those.' He opened a door to a downstairs cloakroom. 'There's a robe in here.'

'And then I'll see you in the drawing room?'

'Yes.'

The robe was a man's short navy-blue towelling. She had wondered if there might be a female robe around, and although this wasn't much of a fit she preferred it. It reached just above her ankles, and gave her the long swinging arms of a gorilla, so she rolled up the sleeves and gathered it in with the belt at the waist.

They had to be friends. That was all she was asking. This time there would be no misunderstandings. She knew a great deal more now. 'I want us to be friends,' she would say. 'Please let us be friends.'

Leon was standing by the drawing room fire. He had taken off his gumboots and his trench coat, and now he was in the open-necked shirt and slacks, barefooted like she was.

Her feet were pink from the hot water she had just washed them in, and she stopped herself saying, 'Snap!' She mustn't be flippant and silly, even if she was nervous. 'Please,' she said, 'I am sorry about this afternoon.'

'It wasn't your fault.' But she was still ashamed of her part in it. 'Sit down,' he said. She took a chair by the fire and he smiled wryly. 'It was in private,' he said. 'She was shown into my office, so there wasn't an audience.'

'There was when she got next door.' She gave a small grimace. 'Uncle Ted had to shut the shop. I was out. When I came back his hair was standing on end.'

Leon laughed, and while he was laughing she asked, 'Do you think it was Judith who phoned her?' He nodded, and she said, 'You're not going to marry Judith, are you?'

'Why not?' But he didn't say he was, and he didn't say it was none of her business.

'I'm sure she'll make a perfectly splendid wife,' she said, 'but I don't see her for you.' The robe was too large. She felt like something soft and vulnerable encased in a protective covering. 'Although Gerald says everyone else does,' she continued lightly.

'Does he?' said Leon. 'Ah well, I can't blame him.'

Why not? Because it was a general opinion, or because he understood why Gerald might try to spoil Fran's friendship with Leon? 'Uncle Ted told me about the birthday card, the one my father wanted me to have.' She need not bring Gerald into this. 'Do you still have it?'

'I'll get it for you.'

She sat trembling, fiddling with the knotted belt of the bathrobe, loosening it a little. It was warm, sitting right by the fire like this.

He brought the card, and he brought a painting, a scene that gave an impression of open spaces, far vistas. 'Is that my father's?' she whispered, and she knew it was, although it was better than any picture he had painted that she had seen. It belonged to the months he was away, and it justified them. He had been growing as an artist when he created this.

Leon put the canvas on a chair and Fran went to kneel

in front of it, drinking in every detail. He said, 'It's for you. I got it last week.'

She remembered his promise, that first night when he took her round the Gallery, and he had remembered it too, and she was overjoyed. No other gift in the world could have delighted her more. She jumped up, flinging her arms around him, stammering, 'Thank you, oh, *thank* you! This is just wonderful. Oh, I just can't tell you how thrilled I am!'

He was smiling, slightly, as though her exuberance amused him. She held him and he looked down at her, and her hands fell from him.

The warmth of her joy faded, and she felt chilled. 'Sorry,' she said. She looked at her hands as though she didn't quite know what to do with them now, or where to put them.

'You don't really want me to touch you,' he said quietly.

But she desperately wanted his arms wrapped around her and she stared. 'Why do you say that?'

'Your mother hates my guts, and so do you.'

'*No.*'

He spoke unhurriedly, he could have been discussing the value of one of the pictures on the wall. There was no sign of emotion in the almost classical face. 'This afternoon she said you might be attracted to me, but you'd never forget that I advised your father to go away. And that's how it is, isn't it? Under your skin I'm always the enemy.'

Fran sat down on the sofa, dropping down, weak at the knees. Somehow she had to make him understand that she was crazy about him, and that went for her subconscious too. But what to say? how to start? Things had gone wrong from the time he made love to her, right here.

She looked down at the sofa, where she sat. 'The last time I was here——' she began.

'Oh yes, I can probably make you want me, I'm fairly adept at lovemaking.' He spoke as though it was a form of athletics. He had the body of a natural athlete, so perhaps it was to him. 'But when I asked if you knew what you were doing you weren't too happy to find yourself in my arms,' he said.

It hadn't been like that. It had been nothing like that. She asked, 'Why did you ask me?'

'I wanted you to say yes, you knew what you were doing.'

She sat up straighter, eyes fixed on him. 'Then you should have looked as though you wanted me to say— yes, I knew, instead of chilly as charity.'

'Did I?' Now there was uncertainty in his voice.

'You did.' There was none in hers. 'Of course I knew where I was and what I was doing, and as for hating you—there's a laugh!'

'Is it?'

She knew then that she must give him the reassurance he needed. That it was all in her hands. She looked at him, straight at him, and said, 'It's as though you've been my lover ever since that first night when Poppy broke down. I've been wanting and loving you ever since. Even when things got snarled up, no matter who I was with——' She paused. 'I missed you,' was not enough. 'I ached for you,' she said. 'Day and night.'

'Do you mean this?' He touched her cheek, his eyes searching hers, and her face crumpled.

'Do I look as though I mean it? How do I look?'

Her love and her need were there for anyone to see

and he sat down beside her, stroking her hair, her face, running his hands down her arms, and beneath the robe holding her close and gently as though to convince himself that she was real. He must have dreamed dreams too.

'I love you,' he said at last.

'I'm glad.' He was a sophisticated man of the world, but his voice was husky, shaking, and Fran said gently, 'Was it that hard to say?'

'Yes.'

'Why?'

He spoke haltingly at first. She said nothing. She nestled beside him, listening, close to him while he told her, 'Perhaps because I never learned to love. My mother died when I was born, and my father never cared for anyone else. Not for me. I'm closer to Ted than I ever was to him, and fonder of Ted.' ... 'Like a son to me' Uncle Ted had said ... 'I've always been on good terms with Ted, especially these last twelve months when the business started to get too much for him, and where Ted is you are. He's always talked about you.'

He smiled at her. 'I knew how you felt about me—the Iceman,' she smiled too, 'but I began to feel that I knew you. Then you told him you were leaving your job because you were having trouble with some man who was jealous, and Ted needed an assistant, and you said you'd come.'

She was so glad that she had come. Dear conniving Uncle Ted was going to be over the moon over this.

'I'd always thought I'd marry Judith some time,' said Leon. 'But I'd never been jealous of Judith, and I suddenly realised that I'd never cared enough about any woman to give a damn if she had a string of lovers.'

Fran moved just enough to slip her arms around his

neck, and hold him so that he had to look at her and smile at her.

'I saw your car turn in the afternoon you arrived,' he told her, 'and I came out. I'd have spoken if you'd smiled, but you didn't.'

'I couldn't then, I thought you were my bad omen.' Instead of the best thing that had ever happened, or could ever happen to her. Her green eyes glinted with tender mischief. 'Are you jealous of me?' He was the first man she had ever wanted to be jealous.

He looked at her as though all the warmth he would ever know must come from her. 'You've set light to me,' he said. 'I can't bear the thought of another man touching you.'

He was due for loving, for warmth and joy and tenderness, and sweet and soaring passion. She kissed his lips and he kissed and kissed her, and then he said, 'Your mother said you'd be leaving with her. I thought you would.'

She shook her head, but he still wasn't quite sure of her. 'She hates me. Could she stop you marrying me?'

She shook her head again, laughing that away, telling him, 'Uncle Ted turned on her this afternoon because of what she said about you. I never heard Uncle Ted shout at anyone before, and Jim's probably spelling out a few home truths right now. She's never going to admit she was to blame for my father leaving us, but they're not going to leave her with any excuse for hating you.'

She was in his arms, her head on one of the big soft cushions, and this house was home because of the man beside her. 'If you're asking me to marry you you'll have me around for the rest of your life.'

'It isn't living without you,' he said. 'It's loneliness and hunger.'

He pulled her closer, until they were locked together without speaking, arms around each other, faces pressed cheek to cheek

She hadn't realised she was weeping with joy until she felt that her cheek was wet. 'This is me crying, isn't it?' she whispered. 'It wouldn't be you?'

He raised his head to look at her. 'It could be me. I never knew I could cry before, but then I never knew I could fall in love. Nothing and nobody but you could make me cry.'

She blinked her damp lashes. 'That's a responsibility.'

'Yes. You do know what you're doing, don't you?'

'I know, my love,' she said, 'I know,' and she pulled him down again beside her.

# Did you miss any of these exciting Harlequin Omnibus 3-in-1 volumes?

## Anne Hampson

**Anne Hampson #3**
Heaven Is High (#1570)
Gold Is the Sunrise (#1595)
There Came a Tyrant (#1622)

## Essie Summers

**Essie Summers #6**
The House on Gregor's Brae (#1535)
South Island Stowaway (#1564)
A Touch of Magic (#1702)

## Margaret Way

**Margaret Way #2**
Summer Magic (#1571)
Ring of Jade (#1603)
Noonfire (#1687)

## Margaret Malcolm

**Margaret Malcolm #2**
Marriage by Agreement (#1635)
The Faithful Rebel (#1664)
Sunshine on the Mountains (#1699)

## Eleanor Farnes

**Eleanor Farnes #2**
A Castle in Spain (#1584)
The Valley of the Eagles (#1639)
A Serpent in Eden (#1662)

## Kay Thorpe

**Kay Thorpe**
Curtain Call (#1504)
Sawdust Season (#1583)
Olive Island (#1661)

# 18 magnificent Omnibus volumes to choose from:

## Betty Neels

**Betty Neels #3**
Tangled Autumn (#1569)
Wish with the Candles (#1593)
Victory for Victoria (#1625)

## Violet Winspear

**Violet Winspear #5**
Raintree Valley (#1555)
Black Douglas (#1580)
The Pagan Island (#1616)

## Anne Hampson

**Anne Hampson #4**
Isle of the Rainbows (#1646)
The Rebel Bride (#1672)
The Plantation Boss (#1678)

## Margery Hilton

**Margery Hilton**
The Whispering Grove (#1501)
Dear Conquistador (#1610)
Frail Sanctuary (#1670)

## Rachel Lindsay

**Rachel Lindsay**
Love and Lucy Granger (#1614)
Moonlight and Magic (#1648)
A Question of Marriage (#1667)

## Jane Arbor

**Jane Arbor #2**
The Feathered Shaft (#1443)
Wildfire Quest (#1582)
The Flower on the Rock (#1665)

# Great value in reading at $2.25 per volume

**Joyce Dingwell**

**Joyce Dingwell #3**
Red Ginger Blossom (#1633)
Wife to Sim (#1657)
The Pool of Pink Lilies (#1688)

**Hilary Wilde**

**Hilary Wilde**
The Golden Maze (#1624)
The Fire of Life (#1642)
The Impossible Dream (#1685)

**Flora Kidd**

**Flora Kidd**
If Love Be Love (#1640)
The Cave of the White Rose (#1663)
The Taming of Lisa (#1684)

**Lucy Gillen**

**Lucy Gillen #2**
Sweet Kate (#1649)
A Time Remembered (#1669)
Dangerous Stranger (#1683)

**Gloria Bevan**

**Gloria Bevan**
Beyond the Ranges (#1459)
Vineyard in a Valley (#1608)
The Frost and the Fire (#1682)

**Jane Donnelly**

**Jane Donnelly**
The Mill in the Meadow (#1592)
A Stranger Came (#1660)
The Long Shadow (#1681)

# Complete and mail this coupon today!